# THE MORALIST OF THE ALPHABET STREETS

Marsh "exhibits the same sophistication and wit that marked her 1988 debut." —*The New York Times*

"a literary masterpiece" —*The Midwest Book Review*

"sylphlike, winningly punctilious…Marsh writes so gracefully and has an acute (if inwardly spiraling) sense of humor." —Ralph Novak in *People*

"a New Yorker who writes like a tar heel and thus gives us this funny novel filled with exuberant tragic characters." —*Library Journal*

"Like Frankie (in Carson McCuller's *The Member of the Wedding*) Marsh's Meredith views the world in a wistful, touchingly idiosyncratic way, while always standing apart from the action she so beautifully renders." —Meg Wolitzer in the *Chicago Tribune*

"Outstanding…This is a book of exceptional warmth and grace. It is entirely engaging in all parts and lingers with the resonance of its deeper messages, presented to us like a platter of fresh fruit on a humid, storm-lowering day." —*Small Press Review*

"packs a punch that is wry and witty as well as, yes, uplifting." —*Metroland* (Albany)

"Marsh's prose is so direct and unfussy that its powerful emotional wallop surprises." —*City Pages* (Minneapolis)

"delightful and surprising." —*Winston-Salem Journal* (North Carolina)

"Splashingly saucy, benevolently brashy, endlessly edgy, devilishly delightful and ravishingly readable." —*The Macon Beacon* (Georgia)

"Fabienne Marsh is a skilled and compassionate writer, who has created complex characters who looks with more than usual perceptiveness into the convoluted nature of family and neighbor- hood relationships." —*Rocky Mountain News* (Colorado)

"In a warm, richly drawn coming-of-age story, a delightfully wry observant 18-year-old with a fondness for frankness and affection-tinged cynicism learns about love and mortality during one important summer." —*Booklist*, Editor's Choice

"Marsh has written a wonderful book. There's a little wisdom in every sentence and laughter on every page. I cried until I laughed." —Michael Lewis, author of *Liar's Poker*

**TRANSATLANTIC AND COAST-TO-COAST ACCLAIM FOR FABIENNE MARSH'S FIRST NOVEL AND NATIONAL BESTSELLER LONG DISTANCES**

"What an impressive debut…Great charm and power and the ability to breathe life into each character. LONG DISTANCES deserves every hyperbole it receives. The reviewer would attempt to add an ornate and spectacular one here, but he is too impa- tient to get back and re-read the book." —*Orange Country Register* (California)

"witty…a charming debut." —*Time Out* (London)

"Strong, wise and entertaining…Marsh's wit is devilish. Her compassion great." —*Boston Herald*

"compulsively readable" —*Chicago Tribune*

"A fresh spin on (the) first novel…" —*The New York Times Book Review*

"Fabienne Marsh uses a respected literary form, the epistolary, seldom seen in contemporary works, with skill, grace and deft effectiveness; she creates a real and likeable family…" —*Pittsburgh Press*

"What makes the novel fascinating is…the technique…By the end of the novel, I felt like a small town postal worker snooping through mail, piecing together my own version of this unfolding drama." —*Charlotte Observer* (North Carolina)

"very funny, touching, and sad all at once" —James Atlas

"A SUPERB FEAT OF MAGIC, A MASTERFUL NOVEL." —*San Mateo Times* (California)

"A surprisingly accomplished effort for a first-time author…" —*ALA Booklist*

"This book is pure magic. I loved reading every page of it. *Long Distances* is the debut of a superb new writer." —Pat Conroy, author of *The Prince of Tides*

"This book is made up of letters and postcards many of which are so accurate they make your skin crawl." —*The Observer* (London)

Literary Editor's Selection (*The Times*, London) A Book-of-the-Month-Club Alternate Selection Washington Square Press Paperback.

# SINGLE, WHITE CAVEMAN

ALSO BY FABIENNE MARSH

*The Moralist of the Alphabet Streets*

*Long Distances*

*Juliette, Rising*

# SINGLE, WHITE CAVEMAN

## Fabienne Marsh

Windtree
Press

©2020 by Fabienne Marsh

All rights reserved. No part of this publication may be reproduced, distributed or transmitted in any form or by any means, without prior written permission.

Send any Rights Requests to:

Windtree Press

https://windtreepress.com/contact

Publisher's Note: This is a work of fiction. Names, characters, places, and incidents are a product of the author's imagination. Locales and public names are sometimes used for atmospheric purposes. Any resemblance to actual people, living or dead, or to businesses, companies, events, institutions, or locales is completely coincidental.

Jacket Design by Mladen Bozic

**Single, White Caveman / Fabienne Marsh**. – 2nd ed.

Print ISBN 978-1-952447-71-6

Ebook ISBN 978-1-952447-72-3

*For single men and women,
past and present.*

# ACKNOWLEDGMENTS

I would like to acknowledge the following readers whose taste, humor and judgment proved unerring.

They are: Louis V. Marsh, Paul C. Marsh, Michele Morris, Kevin Hinchey, Lauren Krenzel, Ellen Lewis, Gus Moreno, Tom Crain, Michael Cader, Barnaby Feder, Todd Krainin, Noel Gunther, Carol Kostik, Tom DeRosa, Fred Thys, Jim Burack and Michael Lewis. Words, even words, cannot express my gratitude.

Others provided muse-like qualities which, however unquantifiable, were nonetheless vital to this effort. They include: Tanya Mohn, Heidi Stamas, Sally Salvatori, Beth Adams, Gail Fishman, Julian Krainin and S.Lane Faison.

# 1

Jim Rosso was anticipating a lonely millennium.

On the advice of his best friend, he requested an application for Smartheart, a dating network limited to Ivy League graduates. Charles Dine, his former roommate from Dartmouth, insisted it was an entertaining and efficient way to meet women. Besides, that's how Charles had met his wife, Rita. If Smartheart could produce a single woman of Rita's caliber, Rosso agreed it was worth a shot.

Aside from Charles's tip, Rosso was sick of advice. In the two years since his divorce, everyone he had ever met, *especially* those miserable in their own affairs, had become the self-appointed expert on his love life. Club Med, Sierra Club, the Hamptons, the Appalachian Trail, cycling though Tuscany, White River rafting, riding the Metroliner, and cruising elevators during rush hour—all these, along with his fifteenth college reunion, were held forth as biospheres for dating. Rosso had only to show up; the environment would do the rest.

Most of the tips were hearsay. With the exception of Rosso's tax attorney, who had met his bride in the elevator, no one had actually tested them. Yet all this liberally dispensed advice was capped with the breezy and infuriatingly winking phrase, "You never know."

Rosso wrestled with his bio, which would appear on the monthly list sent out to members and simultaneously on the web. He had met Doris, his first wife, in college and now resisted taking this impersonal dating method seriously. His first attempt was a shameful form of toe-dipping to test new waters. After reading countless earnest examples of bios provided by Smartheart, all of which contained words like sincere, attractive, nurturing, good communicator and mutual respect, he tossed off the following:

Ex-marine. Womanizer. Detests children and cats.
Perfect Sunday: Beer and ballgames. Likes to fuck.
Millionaire.

In a fit of vicarious bachelorhood, Charles insisted that Rosso translate his bio into French and run it through Smartheart International. That way, it wouldn't really count, Charles explained, since Smartheart's international chapter was separate, chaotic, and mostly comprising female celebrities looking for Arthur Miller types.

To his horror, Rosso received five replies.

"How could any self-respecting woman *possibly* answer such an asshole!?" he asked Charles, who was terrifically curious himself. Rosso's favorite response—and by far the most intelligent—was one from a French woman: "To say that you are a pig is an insult to pigs." In French, it was a *magnificent* put-down, making Rosso wish he had introduced himself in a less offensive manner.

At times like these, a man dusted off his education. Tristan seeks Isolde; Rodolfo seeks Mimi; Paolo seeks Beatrice; or the more direct approach: *Come Live With Me and Be My Love*. All of these, Rosso considered as leads for his bio, then rejected when it became obvious that, with the exception of the passionate shepherd, most of the plots hinged on consumption or death.

The truth about Rosso read more like this: He possessed the quiet confidence of a man who had seen and done just about everything. At five feet eleven inches, with a solid build, he was ruggedly handsome and his brown eyes, in a certain light, looked more like navy blue. His thick brown hair was wavy, with a stubborn cowlick on the back of his head. Rosso's mother claimed he had inherited the cowlick from his father, who had died of a heart attack when Rosso was nine, leaving the book they had been reading together, *The Spirit of St. Louis*, unfinished.

In the end, this is the bio Rosso submitted. He wanted women to know that he was no smoothie. Rusty Romeo or Cave Man Seeks Wife were honest leads. Since he was running over the thirty-five-word limit, he cut out the fact that he had been a military pilot, because, along with his computer work, women might conclude he was a geek.

> Tall, dark, and passionate first-generation (normal) Italian (38). Accomplished hunter-gatherer with undergraduate degree in comparative literature. First marriage ended after a dispute over my passion for both Labs and golf. Seeking feisty, comely, brainy woman with civilizing influence to settle down and raise a family.

Rosso rejected the conventional wisdom about men—that they have a Y chromosome marked egotist; that they are looking to marry their mothers; that they would rather be coddled than challenged; and that, of all the elements in a woman, they are attracted to fire but will eventually settle for water (at room temperature). He would have conceded the Frenchwoman's point about men being pigs. And most men will admit that they don't grow up dreaming of marriage and children. "You held out as long as you could" accompanied by a pat on the back is the tribal response to a man's engagement. But this doesn't mean that men don't take the job seriously once they're hired. Rosso did.

Doris was a painter, a Hampshire College graduate who had won the 1985 Prix de Rome by rendering Carcassonne's medieval fortress in hot pink. At the time, Christo was in vogue and Doris's depiction of Carcassonne's ninth century structure resembled Christo's plan for the wrapping of the Pont Neuf.

When Rosso married Doris, she was making a meager living as a bookbinder in New York City. He was twenty-seven; she was twenty-five. At the time, her rabid hatred of any man, woman, or everyday slob who made a decent wage was amusing. Painters, poets, Buddhists, and Rosso were, of course, exempt. Many of her friends lunched every day at Dean and Deluca in Soho. The one time Rosso was invited, he ended up feeling like Simon in the *Lord of the Flies*—unwelcome and about to be sacrificed. It occurred to Rosso, after scanning the bored, hostile faces of trustfunders dressed in black, that Dean and Deluca's bottom line rested squarely on the very people Doris and her friends reviled. Their savage antipathy towards any profession that required a suit made him an instant outcast, for Rosso was a Brooks Brothers man down to his very boxers.

Rosso knew *everything* about his ex-wife's work.

Each night Rosso listened to Doris's withering doubts about her talent as a bookbinder. He agonized over every glue that was too weak and every spine that had broken.

It was he who took the call from an irate librarian when a first edition of Calvino's *Il Barone Rampante* buckled its spine. Finally, it was he who was left with a fifteen thousand dollar bill for more botched spines when Doris ran off with an outfielder for the Boston Red Sox. Like Doris, the Red Sox are losers—or, at the very least, they have a pathological fear of success. But Rosso loved them both. He couldn't tell you why.

As a divorced man with no children living in Connecticut, Rosso, like all departures from the norm, excited even the dullest imagination. His neighbors watched him mow his lawn, shovel his driveway, wash his storm windows, pick up his mail, and head for New York City in his Ford Explorer, leaving the house too dark for the comfort of New Canaan's Neighborhood Crime Watch. They suspected that Rosso was looking for companionship. Which was true because, in the course of his ten-year marriage, Doris had fleeced him of what she called his "non-essential" friendships.

The first casualty had been David Vimer, Rosso's first-grade buddy who had complimented Doris one too many times on her breasts. Over the years, the list had grown to include Artie, who only had sex with prostitutes, and Bill, who in the fourteen sniffly years Rosso had known him still preferred the back of his hand to a Kleenex.

Rosso told Doris that everyone had "non-essentials," those stray cats of humanity requiring a bowl of milk every now and then. He reminded her that even *she* had *1-800 Mia*, who had convinced Doris of her essentialness by somehow managing to dial their home number in the course of multiple botched suicide attempts. She also had Alan Potter, a Yale dropout, whom Rosso was revolted to learn made a comfortable living as a sperm donor.

Without knowing a thing about James Adams Rosso, everyone on his block had plans for his future. At 4 Hillside, Mrs. Selby was determined to introduce him to her twenty-nine-year-old daughter. Two doors down, at 6 Hillside, Mrs. Morris suspected he was a child molester and wanted him locked up. Across the street, at 7 Hillside, Mr. Williams, a retired oil company manager, hoped to turn him into a golf buddy, and Mrs. Becker, the local real estate saleswoman, wanted his house.

"I can get you seven fifty," she would say, arriving uninvited for her monthly visit.

"Thanks. I'm not selling," Rosso would reply.

"Everybody needs three quarters of a mill."

And, despite Rosso's fantasy about a life free of expensive house repairs, Rosso would tell Mrs. Becker the truth: that he had nowhere else to go.

On the September list, Rosso circled the bios of women living in New York, Massachusetts, and Connecticut. It was an eclectic group and given Rosso's relatively sedate life in the suburbs, Smartheart's list, restocked monthly, held the promise of a new beginning for a gun-shy divorcé.

**Smartheart, Inc. September Listing**
Belle of Amherst with a mind for business (33).
Avid hiker and biker seeks mountain man with the soul of Emerson (Connecticut).

**Smartheart, Inc. September Listing**
Woman who runs with wolves (39). Seeks sensitive, successful man for romantic walks, candlelight dinners, and long-term commitment (New York).

**Smartheart, Inc. September Listing**
California girl (26) transplanted to New England for advanced degree in graphic design. Van Morrison fan. Sexy, spiritual (Connecticut).

**Smartheart, Inc. September Listing**
Barnard graduate (28) and medical doctor in search of Ivy League Lancelot (New York).

**Smartheart, Inc. September Listing**
Freelance writer (34). Young Elizabeth Taylor look-alike seeks boxer-poet. Intense yet soft spot for Elvis (Boston).

Belle of Amherst struck Rosso as either wholesome and employed or a thinly-veiled Type A. Woman Who Runs with Wolves was sentimental and the wolf stuff left him clueless. California girl's self-promotion was odd—especially since the sexiest (not to mention the holiest) people Rosso knew didn't go around proclaiming it. The Barnard doctor was probably a dermatologist or an ER doctor, both of whom Charles would forbid him to date. Like all surgeons, he regarded them as the bottom-feeders of medicine.

Only Elizabeth Taylor sounded worth the trip.

## 2

Charles told Rosso he should play more golf. Not resort golf; local courses, he advised. "It'll get you out."

"It allegedly broke up my marriage," Rosso replied.

"Doris was a whiner," Charles insisted. "If she'd been a good wife, she would have learned as much about golf as you did about typesetting."

"Bookbinding."

"Even more ridiculous."

Charles had a handicap of six, which meant that he could count on an average score of seventy-eight. Since he worked one hundred hours a week, this was no small feat. Rosso admired him. Not just because he was fine golfer but because he was happily married, had two beautiful children, and, by all accounts, was a great surgeon.

Since his divorce, however, Rosso's feelings towards Charles had grown more complicated. For the first time, Rosso had lost his keel and his best friend's future, measured against his own, appeared well-charted and eminently navigable. But far from begrudging Charles his happiness, Rosso was annoyed that

Charles denied him his right to unhappiness. It was as if Charles attributed his divorce to some defect in character. That is, anyone who lacked Charles's discipline, optimism, and self-sufficiency essentially got what he deserved.

Rosso consoled himself with the knowledge that his friend, to some extent, had always been this way. At Dartmouth, Charles, a philosophy major, had once led a discussion about mediocrity and genius. It struck him as unfair that, given the same goal, many people with no talent work all the time and a lucky few, with prodigious amount of genius, work a lot less.

Rosso had been intrigued by Charles's observation but, as often became the case, when he applied it to those he loved, the statement became an insult.

"No amount of genius can make you write, compose, or paint with heart, " Rosso had protested. He spoke in defense of Doris, then his girlfriend of two years.

"True, " Charles agreed. "But heart without genius creates works of sentiment. A Hallmark card."

Rosso had dismissed Charles as narrow-minded, critical, and avoided him for a week. The time away, in the company of much paler characters, produced an infuriating concession on Rosso's part: Charles's pronouncements always seemed to contain an element of truth.

As Rosso and Charles stood on the public course in Connecticut about to tee off, a woman with chestnut hair and eyes so luminous they seemed to steal blue from the sky drove up in a cart, waving and smiling. It was Rita. She hopped out, kissed her husband with a resounding smack, and announced, to the surprise of Charles and to the delight of Rosso, that she was taking up golf.

"I thought you hated it," Rosso said. He leaned over to kiss her on the cheek.

"Did you take a lesson?" Charles asked.

"I can play, honey." She selected a three wood from her new set of clubs. "I know I can play."

Charles was sure the whole thing was a joke. But just after the golfkeeper called for the Dine party, she strode up to the tee and got in position. Rita missed the ball on her first swing, but on her second, she whacked it one hundred yards.

"Good shot!" Charles cried.

"Amazing," Rosso echoed.

Charles took a practice swing, then drove the ball two hundred fifty yards. Rosso took a Mulligan, then sliced into the rough, midway between Rita and Charles.

Charles put his arm around Rita. "Remember that it's a throwing game," he said. "Aim for the upper deck."

"I don't know what you're talking about," she laughed. Two and a half months earlier, Rita had given birth to a baby girl. Their second child. She was breastfeeding and expanding by the moment. "By the ninth hole, my upper deck will completely obstruct my swing." She patted the passenger seat on the golf cart. "Hop in," she added.

"That's okay. I'll walk."

"But I've never driven one of these."

"It's easy." Charles turned to Rosso. "Would you like to ride with Rita?"

"Sure, but I think she wants her husband."

Rosso put his bag on the cart and, for a moment, he and Rita watched Charles make his way down the fairway. He was six feet tall, slender, and walked slowly, casting a long shadow in the late afternoon sun. Either completely relaxed or walking too quickly, he rarely modified his step to suit the rhythm of a place. He had the air of an aristocrat who always seemed to get what he wanted; he just never seemed to *want* the things other men did. When he found people boring, his mind accelerated with witty but often barbed observations, leading others to conclude that he was arrogant. But when he was focused—that is, when he cared about something or somebody—no one could match his charm and sensitivity.

Charles stopped to take a few practice swings and Rita turned to Rosso.

"I married a loner," she said.

"He loves you," Rosso said.

Rita's foot pressed against the accelerator. It was stuck. She looked down and smiled on seeing a fanned pattern of muddy footprints; golfers before her had pumped the cart's pedal in frustration. When the pedal engaged, a comforting hum lulled her back into her own thoughts. Prints in the snow, she remembered. It had been her second date with Charles nine years earlier. He had picked her up in a cab. They were in New York City heading towards Lincoln Center. The Philharmonic was playing Mozart's *Requiem*. Charles's sister, Mary, who would be singing in the choir, had given him tickets. Charles had caught Rita's eye and said, "I come from a good family. My parent's celebrate their forty-second wedding anniversary next week."

Rita had thought about this line as the cab, with chains on its tires, made its way slowly and rhythmically across Central Park. Above them, branches laden with snow made an airy cage of lace while, below, the blinding powder bleached purity back into the landscape. Rita and Charles had been awed by the scene. It was magical, conferring beauty and grace on all city dwellers who made their way silently through the snow.

At the corner of Broadway and 66th street, Rita had stumbled as Charles helped her out of the cab.

"I'm sorry," she had said, looking down at the print she had made.

"Size seven," Charles said quickly, examining the tread.

"Seven and a half," she had corrected.

"Nine and a half. Narrow," Charles said, stamping his boot next to hers.

She had looked up and smiled, disarmed by his playfulness.

Rita drove the cart up to her ball, which had missed the fairway and was three inches into the rough. As she pulled out her five wood, she thought about how the universe of time she and Charles had enjoyed during their courtship had been swallowed up by their daily responsibilities. Their most relaxing outings had become, for Rita, logistical nightmares. To play golf, she'd had to pump a full hour to obtain three bottles of milk. Then her sitter had canceled, forcing her to scramble for a high school girl she didn't know as well. During the hours she should have been napping, she had watched every golf video the local library owned. And just now, her letdown was starting: the tingling sensation, followed by an insistent pinch meant that, somewhere, her baby was crying. It was like wearing a parole anklet, except, in this case, the baby was the warden.

"Do you really think so?" Rita asked, revisiting Rosso's comment as she hit the ball.

"Think what?" Rosso said, admiring her ball in flight.

"That he loves me?"

Rita's ball landed just short of the green.

Rosso turned towards Rita. "I know it," he said.

"How are you so certain of something I don't feel?"

Rita put her club back in the bag and slid on the seat next to Rosso. He studied her exquisite features with the gentle curiosity of a naturalist spotting his rarest animal—her large eyes, her impetuous full lips, her strong, agile body. Charles had really hit the jackpot with Rita.

"He's always talking about you and planning what to get you for all the sentimental holidays," Rosso said.

Rita drove up to his ball and watched Rosso pitch onto the green. As he slid his club into the bag, he took a moment to prepare his story.

"Can you keep a secret?" Rosso asked.

Rita locked an imaginary lock and threw her arm as if to fling away the key.

"He drew a red heart around your name when he first got your Smartheart bio."

"Really?" Rita smiled.

He saw Charles approach. "It gets better," Rosso whispered quickly. "He *never* requested another bio, and he *refused* to date anyone else."

"How do you know?"

"Because I tried to set him up."

Since the day was devoted to golf, Rosso gave Rita the abbreviated version of a story whose afterlife had continued to haunt him.

New York City had been expecting a blizzard the night Charles had summoned Rosso to the Oak Bar. Rosso, who had arrived late, could still picture the woman who was eyeing Charles. He had even encouraged Charles to pursue her. But Charles, who had only known Rita two weeks, was not interested. Instead, he announced he was taken. "I've met the woman I'm going to marry."

Rita seized upon Rosso's story to forgive Charles. As he approached, she was imbued with love for her husband.

With his foot, Charles tapped Rita's ball onto the fairway. "Take it from here, honey," he said hurriedly. He stared at her as she tried once, twice, then a third time to hit the ball. Finally, she leaned on her club and smiled sweetly at her husband.

"I need a coach," she said.

"You're doing fine," he said.

"Tell me what I'm doing wrong," she pleaded. She had eavesdropped on men at the driving range and knew them to be capable of exchanging golfing tips with the hushed reverence of women consorting over the latest wrinkle cream.

"You need to take a lesson," he said.

After Rita missed the ball, she turned to Rosso. "What am I doing wrong?"

"Try to keep your head down," he said quietly.

With that, Rita hit the ball one foot shy of the green.

"Nice!" came the collective cry.

Rita was encouraged. "Ride with me, honey!" she said, smiling at Charles. "You're in the presence of a champion."

The next hole went slowly. At one point, Charles asked Rita to pick up her ball.

"How come?" Rita asked.

Charles pointed to an elderly man approaching in a cart with the word "Marshal" emblazoned across the roof.

"What's a golf marshal?" she asked.

"He keeps track of time."

"Am I holding everybody up?"

"We're slow," Charles said.

"But there's no one behind us!"

"Doesn't matter. We're running late."

"We're late, we're late, for a very important date," Rita muttered, picking up her ball.

"Did you say something?" he asked.

"I was wondering if this leisurely game that's supposed to bring couples together promises to be one more source of tension and pressure."

"Not if we're not late."

Charles's smug little double negative grated on Rita's nerves.

"C'mon. Hop in," he said. His foot was poised on the accelerator. His eyes were fixed on the green, where he only had to execute a simple putt.

From a few yards away, Rosso saw Charles run over Rita's foot. She bent down to rub her ankle and Rosso caught up with her. Charles kept on riding.

They watched Charles putt though and par without them. "How bout that!?" he cried.

Rita hobbled to her next shot, dropping the ball where Rosso's shot had landed. She missed and dug up a toupee of grass.

Charles drove back towards them. "Hop in," he said to Rita. Rosso saw Rita wiping tears from her eyes.

"What's the matter?" Charles asked.

"What's the *matter*?!" Rita cried.

"Why the tears?"

"You run over my foot, you don't check it, and you finish the hole without us."

"So?"

"So, it's lousy golf etiquette, not to mention the fact that you're supposed to be a *doctor*."

"I didn't know I'd run you over."

"How could you? You're a robot!"

"You ran her over," Rosso interrupted. "Apologize."

"She's not moving fast enough."

"She just had a baby, *asshole* !"

"I didn't ask her to come out here!"

"Well, be *fucking* glad she *did*!"

"Let's have a look," Charles said. He lifted his wife onto the cart and pressed her ankle gently.

"Does that hurt?" he asked.

"No."

"Can you walk on it?"

"Yes."

"You're exhausted," he said. "Let's go home."

"It's not the golf that's exhausting me."

"What is?"

"I can't get you out of bed for a night feeding, but some retiree in a golf hat driving a tin truck and calling himself Marshal has you goose-stepping!"

"There are rules to every game—"

"And exceptions to those rules!"

By this time, the marshal was careening towards them to see if Rita was okay. Charles thought he was trying to advance the game, but Rosso knew better. "Scram," he yelled from a few yards away. He was about to say something more forceful until an embarrassed Rosso recognized the marshal as Mr. Williams, his retired neighbor who volunteered on the course in exchange for free rounds of golf. Rosso apologized and made Mr. Williams understand that he would explain the matter another time.

"Don't you miss married life?" Rita asked Rosso.

Charles said nothing—his habit when Rita got emotional. On those occasions, she was never more vocal.

"I'll tell you what *else* is the matter," Rita said. "You're *never* late for rounds, for the operating room, or for golf, but you're *always* late for me if you show up *at all*, and I spend my life *waiting!*"

The sad truth, which became abundantly clear to Rosso at that moment, was that Rita's needs, however worthy, would always be competing with life and death, with aneurysms, gunshot wounds, and vehicular traumas.

"Let's call it a day," Charles said.

"I want to finish this hole, " Rita insisted.

"I've had enough."

"Help me off the cart!"

Charles went around to the passenger side and dipped his shoulder to support her. She walked over to her ball while Charles headed for the green to tend the flag.

Rita practiced her grip, waggled a bit, and held her pitching iron as if it were a divining rod. She waited until her husband was out of range, then whacked the ball. Just as Charles was turning to observe his wife's shot, a Pinnacle 2 hit him squarely on the temple.

# 3

Every so often, a message on Rosso's screen would remind him to contact the September crop—especially Belle of Amherst, Elizabeth Taylor, and California Girl. He had held off for a month because he was intimidated. Rosso realized that he suffered from a form of social paralysis: one so rare that it struck only divorced men and women; one so severe that it caused their dating skills to atrophy. The condition also produced a time warp. Rosso knew his chronological age to be thirty-eight, but he suspected that in single years, he was barely twenty-eight. He lacked guile and was trusting to the point of idiocy.

In this period of self-doubt, Rosso received an e-mail from California girl.

*I liked your bio. Why didn't you request mine?*
*I'll attach it.*
*Don't be a stranger.*

Rosso downloaded her bio.

FABIENNE MARSH

**Smartheart Inc.**

**Name:** Phoebe Larsen

**Schools:** Brown University, B.A. (Fine Arts)

**Address:** 16 Orchard Drive, New Canaan, Connecticut

**Age:** 26. **Height:** 5'7"

**Description:** Blonde, blue-eyed California girl.

**Status:** Single

**Children:** None

**Religion:** My own brand

**Hobbies (in order of importance):** Meditation, mountain biking, cats, Van Morrison, yoga, snow skiing.

**Favorite Books:** *The Road Less Traveled* (my favorite poem too!), *Lust for Life* (about Vincent Van Gogh), and anything about Wilhelm Reich.

**What are you looking for in a companion?:** Honesty, kindness, intelligence, spirituality, and fitness.

Just as Rosso was contemplating what Phoebe could possibly have meant by "Religion: My own brand," he was interrupted by a series of calls.

The first was from Charles, who was with Rita at St. John's, his own hospital, awaiting lab results for the blow to his head.

"You've got to get me out of here!" he cried. "These crystal-waving medicine men won't let me operate!"

"Play Scrabble with Rita," Rosso advised. "That's what Bill and Hillary do."

He knew that Charles hated "I feel your pain" Democrats as much as he despised Alan Alda, Lamaze classes, and group hugs. Surgeons, he had learned, were a special breed: They ate nails with their oatmeal, which nourished an iron resolve. If they were sick, they wouldn't admit it. If they were troubled, they simply pushed on. They couldn't eat, piss, or emote for inhumane periods of time. Rosso compared them to the Navy Seals of medicine, so exacting was the discipline, skill, and, sometimes, the emotional detachment required.

With all this contempt for the weak, the irony was that Charles was reputed to have a great deal of compassion for his patients. He wanted to get back to work.

Charles handed Rita the phone. "He's impossible," she told Rosso. She had sat by her husband's side, listening to him rant, and watched him finger his beeper as if it were a set of prayer beads. She thought about how she had come to *loathe* that beeper. At night, it lay beside their phone with a second beeper for traumas parked next to it. Her daughter's bassinet was a few yards away and her son's room was within earshot.

The night before they had played golf, she had put Tina to bed at 10 p.m., then had gone to bed at eleven. Charles had come in at eleven thirty and they had talked about his cases until twelve. The trauma beeper went off at 12:45 a.m. Charles called the hospital. Five gunshots to the chest. Dead on arrival. He went back to sleep. The beeper kept on chirping, but Charles was too tired to hear.

"Clear your beeper," Rita had moaned. She finally got back to sleep, then the phone rang. The baby woke up soon after at 3 a.m. Rita fed her and went back to bed at 3:30 a.m. The baby cried and cried. Rita nursed her and went back to sleep, only to be awakened by the other beeper at four thirty. Charles made two more calls. At 5:00 a.m., his alarm went off. At six thirty, Daniel woke up because he heard his father leave. By 7:30, Tina was awake.

She did the math. If Charles had not come home, Rita would have had a blissful and much needed eight hours of sleep. Instead, she had an interrupted three and a half hours. Charles's career was her newborn and the beeper was its insistent cry.

This accumulation of sleep deprivation left her both hating her life and unqualified to advise Rosso on matters of the heart. On a happier note, she told Rosso that she had landed a part-time job.

"Doing what?" he asked.

"I'm too embarrassed to tell you," she had said. "I haven't even told Charles."

After Rosso had finished with Charles and Rita, Doris called to offer him tickets to a Red Sox game. At first he was pissed. He wanted to tell Doris to tell her benchwarmer where to stick his tickets. At the same time, Rosso was perplexed. Doris had never given him tickets to anything, and these days they almost never talked. Still, she said there were a few "minor" changes in her life. For starters, she had given up bookbinding which somehow, he admitted, broke his heart. The decision was a relief to Doris, which made him wonder why the news left him feeling like a failure.

There was also some wonderful news. Doris had started to paint again, which came as a complete surprise. Rosso suppressed his instinctive reaction—which was to be jealous of the Red Sock who was obviously proving to be a better muse for Doris than he—and asked her what she wanted him to do with the twenty-seven canvases he was storing in both his bedroom closet and her former studio.

"Have a garage sale," she said breezily. "I've improved a lot."

"What about the Prix de Rome!?"

"Keep anything you like."

Oh. Okay. Just like that, Rosso thought. And, by the way, the other "minor" change was the fact that Doris was three months pregnant. Of all the news, this was the most devastating.

Rosso had wanted children desperately and, other than the disputes over Labrador Retrievers and golf, it was their only major issue. Doris had been resolute. She didn't know who she was, she had said; and she had not discovered herself professionally. Children would have to wait. Now that Rosso's angry rebel had turned thirty-six. Now that his formerly surly beauty was taking real estate courses in neighboring Westchester County and studying to be a broker. Now that his would-be bookbinder had been impregnated by a Red Sock, he was forced to confront the sad, ego-bruising possibility that Doris hadn't simply not wanted children. Maybe she had never wanted children with *him*.

He couldn't even console himself with the artistic "canvas children" she had birthed in the course of their relationship because, after moving out, his ex-bride was now experiencing the kind of creative torrent known only to Georgia O'Keefe *after she'd moved to the fucking desert!*

All this was too much to bear. And it made Rosso long to be a pig. Because the truth was that the pigs got all the girls. He didn't know what that said about pigs, and he wouldn't venture to guess what it said about girls.

Before leaving for the office, Rosso reached Phoebe, the California Girl, online. Since she was state-of-the art, Phoebe had included a photograph of herself. Rosso was far from repulsed.

JR: Hello.
P: Hello.
JR: Thanks for sending your bio.
P: You're welcome. Why didn't you request mine?

JR: I did.
P: Really?
JR: Yes. I was going to contact you, but your bio wasn't available. You've got some nice computer equipment.
P: It's my field. Can you send me a picture?
JR: I don't have one on file.
P: Do you have a scanner?
JR: Yes.
P: Scan yourself.
JR: What?
P: Put your face against the scanner and send. I want to see what you look like.
JR: Are you serious?
P: Yes.

Rosso pressed his face against the scanner.

P: You either need a new head or a new scanner.
JR: What happened?
P: I think you should try again.
JR: I feel like an idiot.
P: Much better. You're cute. I knew you would be. A lot of the guys say they're handsome and they're toads. One guy lied about his height.
JR: By how much?
P: Four inches.
JR: No!
P: Another said he had brown hair when he had no hair.
JR: C'mon.
P: The worst one had his ears done.
JR: Why?
P: They stuck out.
JR: A male bimbo.
P: No, he was smart. He just wasn't as spiritual as I am.

Rosso hesitated. He decided to give Phoebe the benefit of the doubt.

> JR: What faith?
> P: It's not a church or temple religion. I meditate every morning. Do you?
> JR: No. Should I?
> P: Everyone should. It's cool.

Rosso looked at her picture. She really was gorgeous.

> JR: What isn't cool?
> P: The Military.
> JR: What do you mean The Military?
> P: The Military Industrial Complex.
> JR: What about it?
> P: It's not cool.
> JR: I'm a former Navy pilot.
> P: Top Gun?
> JR: Yeah.
> P: That's very cool.
> JR: Explain to me how The Military can't be cool when Top Gun can.
> P: Because of the movie.
> JR: I see. You're funny.
> P: I wasn't trying to be.
> JR: You weren't?
> P: No.
> JR: You're serious?
> P: Yes.
> JR: Are you reading any Eisenhower?
> P: Who?
> JR: The guy who coined the term military-industrial complex.

P: I saw *JFK*. That's where I heard it. Have you seen Oliver Stone's *JFK*?
JR: Yes.
P: It was a masterpiece.
JR: Did you really go to Brown?
P: Why?

*Because you're dimmer than a forty-watt bulb!* He told Phoebe that she was a sweet, beautiful woman, but that he did not want to waste her time. Then he signed off.

A few minutes later the message icon on his laptop started blinking.

*I like smart men. That's why I called you. Some of the stupidest people I know went to Ivy League schools. I'm not stupid. Give me a chance.*

## 4

Rosso's in-flight snack lay trapped under cellophane in its wicker basket. He stared at the granola bar, the box of raisins, the packet of processed cheese, the container of orange juice, and the tiny Delicious apple. He would need a pen to set them free.

He slid open his window blind and peered down at the ocean. No land in sight. Rosso's last trip to the Bahamas had been with Doris. They had stayed at the Ocean Club, a small resort on Paradise Island with clay tennis courts and an enormous pool set like a jewel in the gardens of a twelfth century Cistercian cloister. Hibiscus had grown everywhere. Their red and yellow flutes greeted visitors like miniature gramophones, but the only sounds within earshot had been bird calls and the occasional pock of a well-hit tennis ball. The hotel, a restored plantation house, stood on a bluff under which a beach was nestled. As far as the eye could see, there was sand the color of nougat and water the searing blue of tourmaline.

At the time of Rosso's visit, the new 18-hole golf course had been under construction. This was the course Rosso had come to play; the International Encryption Association conference offered an excuse.

As Rosso reached into his briefcase, he scanned the passengers making their way down the aisle. How could my fellow Americans be so fat? Man after man, child after child, mother after mother—one after another, with the exception of a woman who smiled at Rosso and retreated behind the First Class curtain.

Rosso retrieved his Uni-ball Micro Point and jabbed the snack basket's membrane so vigorously that he punctured the foil sealing the orange juice. He pressed the call button. When the flight attendant arrived, she said, "We made a mess, didn't we?" in the singsongy voice of a preschool teacher. Minutes later, she returned with napkins and wiped the tray table with a fury that spilled more orange juice, this time on Rosso's lap.

"Ah!" he cried, feeling the liquid penetrate his khakis. Before he could stop her, the attendant had grabbed his neighbor's club soda, ice and all, and dumped it on Rosso's crotch.

"What are you doing!?"

"Cutbacks," she explained crisply. "The airline no longer pays for dry cleaning."

Rosso waved away the attendant and patted himself dry with a blanket. When no one was looking, he aimed two air jets at his lap and cast a reproachful look at the apple that had enticed him in the first place. After his body had warmed to cabin temperature, he booted up his computer and reviewed the notes for his presentation. It was Rosso's job to see that a company's firewalls, or electronic fences, were secure. Hackers received the most press for stealing credit card numbers and commandeering phone lines, but aside from the occasional logic bomb, most of the exposures Rosso dealt with were less dramatic—viruses, internal hacking, and, less frequently, tracking down the source of a scouring flame.

After he developed sinus problems, Rosso switched from

Navy Pilot to Intelligence. He was grateful to the military for teaching him computers and, specifically, how to guard secret data. Yet for as long as he could remember, Rosso's dream had been to fly. He was drawn to the sky as instinctively as a dog's snout seeks an open window. At first, Rosso had pictured himself in an *F14 Tomcat* . Since it meant living on an aircraft carrier for six months with six thousand men, he chose instead the *P3 Orion*—a big, land based, multi-engine aircraft used to hunt submarines.

For the Navy, men like Rosso were maddening. They were among the best reason to stay in the military. After eighteen weeks in Aviation Officer Candidate School, where he swam a mile in his flight suit, was dragged at high speed behind a PT boat, and survived a simulated helicopter crash, Rosso went on to Naval Flight School in Pensacola, Florida. Two years later, with hundreds of flight hours logged, he was forced to quit when his sinuses could no longer equalize pressure changes in the cabin.

With help from Doris, who'd been his fiancé at the time, and a few leads into the highly paid world of security consulting, Rosso eased back into civilian life. Five months after leaving the Navy, he was headhunted by Bob Hersh, a venture capitalist who had started his own software business. Hersh's exuberance, generosity, and determination proved winning. In 1988, Rosso joined Future Systems, a small company specializing in defensive software.

At the Ocean Club, Future Systems would be introducing defensive software which promised to improve firewall security well into the twenty-first century. As a troubleshooter and consultant to blue-chip companies, Rosso reviewed network topography and identified possible entry points. Satisfied that his notes and slides were in order, he read one chapter in a brilliant biography of John D. Rockefeller, two chapters in a novel about fly-fishing, and one speech by his beloved Churchill, whose memoirs he had read, re-read, and sometimes recited in the shower.

After that, he punched up a new crop of bios he had downloaded from the Smartheart website.

**Smartheart, Inc. October Listing.**
Portfolio Manager (32). I went to Smith and have "A Century of Women On Top" T-shirt to prove it, but call me old-fashioned becuase I enjoy the company of men (Hartford).

Rosso checked out her bio.

**Smartheart, Inc.**

**Name:** Susan Marshall

**Occupation:** Portfolio Manager

**Schools:** Smith College; B.A. in English (Romantic Poets)

**Address:** 58 Mountain Road, West Hartford, Connecticut.

**Age:** 32. **Height:** 5'6"

**Description:** Blonde hair; blue eyes.

**Status:** Single

**Children:** None

**Religion:** Methodist

**Hobbies (in order of importance):** Conversation, Goethe Society and Japanese tea ceremony.

**Favorite Books:** *The French Lieutenant's Woman*

**What are you looking for in a companion?** Honesty, kindness, intelligence.

Perfect for someone, Rosso thought, but too earnest and too boring for him. Besides, green tea tasted like piss.
He went on to the next.

**Smartheart, Inc. October Listing.**
Investment Banker/Standup Comic (29). I will support you and make you laugh. All you have to do is be 62.78 percent certifiably normal (*Is that so hard?*) (New York City).

Rosso worried he might come up short on her normalcy calculation, but since he liked women with good senses of humor, he called up her bio.

**Smartheart, Inc.**

**Name:** Gina Bonaventura

**Occupation:** Investment Banker/Comedienne

**Schools:** Massachusetts Institute of Technology; Ph.D. in Economics

**Address:** 14 Prince Street, New York City

**Age:** 29. **Height:** 5'4

**Description:** Brown hair with pink stripe on weekends; brown eyes with purple contacts on weekends.

**Status:** Divorced

**Children:** Don't want any.

**Religion:** Hate 'em all.

**Hobbies (in order of importance):** Comedy clubs, Rollerblading, any movie by Albert Brooks.

**Favorite Books:** *The 2000 Year-old Man* (if I have to explain, you're not for me).

**What are you looking for in a companion?** I know it when I see it.

A little too out there, Rosso thought. The kind of woman who would deliberately give you a neck full of hickeys on the eve of an important meeting and think it was funny.
He pulled up the last bio.

**Smartheart, Inc. October Listing.**
Concert Flautist (37). Juilliard grad who wants to raise a musical family, but who has no interest in dating musicians (Brooklyn).

Rosso suspected that the flautist's joys were far too subtle for a boor like himself. Anyone who has seen a string quartet or even two musicians playing a duet in that half-smiling state of tacit, knowing, and *obscene* ecstasy would understand Rosso's position, but in the spirit of you-never-know-ness, he gave her a shot.

**Smartheart, Inc.**

**Name:** Jeanette Mandel

**Occupation:** Musician/Flautist

**Schools:** Juilliard School of Music and The Peabody Institute (Baltimore)

**Address:** 15 Henry Street, Brooklyn

**Age:** 37. **Height:** 5'9"

**Description**: light-brown hair, light-brown eyes

**Status:** Divorced

**Children:** Wonderful nine year old

**Religion:** Jewish, but enjoy Unitarian services

**Hobbies (in order of importance):** Music in performance; anything by Rampal or the Guarneri String Quartet.

**Favorite Books:** Arthur Rubenstein's autobiography; Auguste Renoir's biography by his son.

**What are you looking for in a companion?** Sensitivity, responsibility, and someone who can't live without music.

 Great books, good woman, Rosso thought. But definitely too sensitive for him.
 Rosso heard a snore from across the aisle and turned towards the honker. Sleeps with her mouth open, he observed.

Very unattractive. He bit into the apple he suspected was bred for airplane snackpacks. Just as he was finishing it, the flight attendant asked Rosso to prepare for landing and dipped her plastic bag to receive the apple's core. From the window, he saw the tart green fairways of the Ocean Club, flanked by a deserted beach.

Rosso shared an open-air taxi with a couple from New Jersey and their two children. At the last minute, a young woman hopped in. She was the smiler from First Class.

The driver bounced over rutted roads and careened past natives on foot. Five minutes into the ride, he stopped by a palm tree to pick up his friend, who handed him a basket of fruit in exchange for the ride.

The smiles of the young woman sharing Rosso's taxi grew more impertinent until, finally, she blurted out, "You look familiar." A nearby tree rustled in the breeze and the sharp Caribbean light cut its shade like swords. Rosso squinted to get a better look at the woman. Bouncy hair, bouncy body, bouncy smile. He reached for his baseball cap, suddenly conscious of the need to cover his still-damp khakis.

The woman laughed. "It's okay. I saw what happened."

Rosso smiled. He was flattered that the woman from First Class had somehow managed to observe him from behind the great polyester divide, but Rosso found himself incapable of small talk. On the outskirts of Nassau was a small restaurant. He stared at the porch where he and his wife had eaten dinner and was overcome with sadness.

When Rosso arrived at the reservations desk, the concierge handed him a message. The bellhop took his luggage and led him to a modest room in the new golf villas. Once inside, Rosso set up his laptop, stacked his books on the night table, and fumbled for his phone card; the two dollar surcharge for long distance calls violated his sense of fair play. He pulled back the curtains and lay on the bed as his call went through. The line crackled but the voice was unmistakably that of Jeff Reed, the Future Systems expert on cryptographic software.

"How's the weather?"

"Nice," Rosso said. He turned on the television and looked out the floor-to-ceiling window. He had waited five years to play the brand new, perfectly groomed, eighteen-hole golf course.

"See if you can get a 7 a.m. tee time for Sunday," Jeff said. He wanted to squeeze in nine holes before the conference began.

Rosso called the pro shop and stared out the window. There may not be women, he sighed to himself, but there would always be golf, CNN, Churchill, and his Bobby Orr video.

Soon after Rosso hung up, he heard a knock at his door. It was the smiler from the open-air taxi.

"I know who you are!" she said. "You're Jimmy Rosso!" Her smile was clean and clear as a shot from space. "I'm Michelle O'Hare. I went to Our Lady of Fatima with your sister, *Elaine!*"

Michelle had filled out considerably in the years after graduating.

"The Midge doll," Rosso said, remembering. "You always took the Barbie doll and made Elaine play with Midge."

The childhood memory comforted Rosso but, moments later, the sight of Michelle began to unsettle him. Gone was her parochial school innocence. In form, figure, face, and manner, she had grown into a major-league bombshell.

Rosso's first days at the Ocean Club were less about golf than sex with Michelle. Despite his ironclad tee times, Rosso found himself in bed with Michelle in the morning, or at lunch, or sometimes during Michelle's four o'clock chocolate hour. Failing that, during cocktail hour, or just before dinner, but *no sex after dinner*. Aside from that one rule, there was nothing

Michelle would not try and no position, however acrobatic, from which she shied away.

Eighteen hours into the lovemaking, it was clear that Rosso's golf stretches were insufficient training for these marathons. He threw in a few groin and back stretches, but he was still sore. Michelle seemed to require the employment of every available muscle in his body.

"Are you always like this?" Rosso asked. He was making small talk in order to give himself a breather.

"You bring it out in me," she said.

"Maybe we should rest."

"Why? "

"Because I'm an old man."

Michelle reached for the remote and straddled Rosso's buttocks. "What are you doing?"

"Giving the old man a massage," she said, flipping to the *E!* channel to watch a show on fashion emergencies.

Rosso suddenly wondered why a young, beautiful woman would come to a resort by herself. "Don't you have any girlfriends?"

"Yes," she laughed. "But now we play with Ken dolls."

On the second night, after cutting his golf game short to meet her, Rosso was put off when Michelle casually mentioned that she had an appointment with "another guy." She said. "No big deal."

"What do you mean no big deal? " Rosso asked, suddenly worried that his reckless behavior might have bacterial or viral consequences.

"Oh relax!" Michelle cried, sounding a bit irritated. "It's just my husband."

"Your HUSBAND?"

"Yeah, my husband."

"You're married? "

"Yes."

He glanced at her left hand. "You don't wear a ring!"

"It's in the safety deposit box."

"You know my sister! How could you lie to me!?"

"I felt sorry for you."

"*Sorry* for me!?"

"I remember when your father died."

"That was thirty years ago!"

"I haven't seen you since."

"You have sex with men you feel sorry for?"

"Not usually."

"What do you do usually?"

"Have sex with my husband."

"I'M YOUR FIRST AFFAIR!?"

"It doesn't count. You're the brother of a childhood friend."

"What's so brotherly about what we've been doing!?

Rosso paced back and forth in his Ocean Club robe. "What time did your husband tee off yesterday?"

"Two fifty-five."

"Christ, he was my fourth!"

"Really?"

"And he was my fourth *today!*" Rosso wailed. "*He's a great guy!*"

"Of course he is!"

"Sam."

"That's right."

"I leave Sam standing on the green to make love to his wife and *he's a great guy!*"

"I said he was."

"So what's the matter with you!?"

"What do you mean?"

"You've got a great husband and you cheat on him."

"I told you. It doesn't count."

"For me, it *counts!*" Rosso cried. "I don't have sex with married women, especially with golfers' wives!"

"What's the matter with golfers' wives?"

"Nothing. It violates my code."

Michelle tried to persuade Rosso that it wasn't his fault, but Michelle's husband didn't see it that way. On Sunday evening, after a four-course, five-star dinner in the plantation courtyard with his wife, Sam strode up to the table where Rosso and Jeff were having dinner. He asked Rosso to get up, whereupon Sam, whose huge, muscular body seemed better suited for a rotating dais, took one swing and gave Rosso a fat lip.

He didn't seem to want to do it.

Rosso did not want him to do it.

Michelle did not want it done.

It was ritualistic brutality, from which no one drew any pleasure. If anything, both men were irritated by Michelle's foul play and her lack of respect for their gentlemen's code.

The next day, which happened to be the first day of the conference, Rosso and Jeff took to describing his injury as a freak golf accident, which, to their surprise, drew a great deal of sympathy. Despite Rosso's grotesquely swollen lip with an unsightly cut where Sam's Notre Dame ring had made contact, the conference was a resounding success and Rosso went home with a new Scotty Cameron putter—a gift from Bob Hersh, the chairman of Future Systems.

# 5

Rosso landed in Newark. He had promised to visit his mother, so he rented his first Beetle and drove to Montclair. On the way, he picked up an ice pack. His lip was killing him. If he didn't get the swelling down, his mother would have kittens.

As he pulled into the driveway of her condo, Rosso saw his sixty- six- year-old mother wave from behind the storm window. In appearance, Flora bore a striking resemblance to England's Queen Mother during the war years. Her sweet, grandmotherly demeanor concealed an inner fire. She was a survivor, with the hardscrabble determination of a commoner. Her periwinkle suit with a matching hat signaled that she considered the lunch a special occasion. She wanted to go to Zambini's, her favorite restaurant.

Then she saw the lip.

"What *happened* to you?"

"Golf injury. I'm fine."

"You're not fine. You've got lips like a London broil. Are you playing hockey again?"

"No."

"Can you eat?"

"Sure."

Two hours later, over dessert, sometime between the strawberry and chocolate of her *spumoni*, Rosso sensed a change in his mother's mood. She began pestering him about Maria Movado, a woman she had set him up with two years before.

"Old news, Mom," Rosso said, digging into his *tartufo* .

"You never called her again. How could a son of mine be so rude?" Easy, Rosso thought.

Smart, funny, pretty, and successful is how his mother had described the thirty-four-year-old daughter of her bridge partner. Yet the date had been a disaster. Maria's pale face, crimson lipstick, and black leather cape made her look like a vampire—which proved all the more menacing when her conversation turned out to be a narcotic. Brown, the new black, had been replaced by gray, which had deposed red to become the new brown. So *black*, Maria had explained, was now back to *black*, and she had been the first consultant in the fashion industry to predict the trend.

"She wasn't for me. Let's leave it at that," Rosso said firmly.

His mother didn't know the half of it. The part that embarrassed even Rosso on recollection was that, after dessert, Maria had asked him to watch *Field of Dreams*. Since the film was based on *Shoeless Joe*, one of his favorite baseball stories, he agreed. Two hours later, in Maria's loft on Broome Street, during the catch between the father and son, when Rosso's eyes started to mist, Maria had put the film on pause.

"Are you *crying!?*" she had asked.

Rosso, who was wholly absorbed in what he would have been the first to concede was a male weepie, suddenly felt Maria studying his face.

"No," Rosso replied, confident that his eyes had the structural integrity of the Hoover Dam.

"I think you *are!*" Maria insisted. She punched the stop

button and, for a rare moment, appeared animated. Why, she wanted to know, had the scene moved him?

Since Rosso had sat through *Gone With the Wind* and *Terms of Endearment* dozens of times without ever *once* interrupting a film, ridiculing a woman about her emotions, or commandeering a remote, he was irritated by Maria's lack of sensitivity.

"My mother told me that your father died when you were young," Maria had said casually. When Rosso did not respond, she added, "It must be a father-son thing."

"Must be," Rosso said.

Rosso's statement, if only for a second, seemed to resolve Maria's internal debate over the legitimacy of Rosso's feelings. But when she started up again, Rosso grabbed his coat and left. He was not in the mood to have his emotions analyzed in the virulent, neurotic Petri dish of Maria's psyche.

On the way to his car, Rosso had concluded that he had no future as a dater. He would rather get a dog. A dog would understand what Maria never could. It boiled down to this. How do you explain to anyone, let alone a woman you hardly knew, that you feel your father's presence in every cloud, every rainbow, every well-oiled machine, and every catcher's mitt?

"Fine. So who *is* for you!?" Rosso's mother persisted.

"Right now, nobody."

"Suddenly you're picky!" she shouted, pressing her palms together. "You married *Doris* and *now* you're picky?"

Rosso watched his mother do what she had done countless times during his childhood. She clasped her hands, looked towards the heavens, and invoked his father's presence. It drove him crazy. Worse still, his mother would interpret his father's reactions.

"How do you think your father feels," she said. "Looking down and seeing a *meshuga*!"

"Meshuga?"

"It means nut."

"I know what it means. You don't speak Yiddish. Dad doesn't either."

"What's the matter with you?" Rosso asked. His mother had never attacked him like this.

"You married a flake. That makes you a nut. I don't want you to make the same mistake."

"Fine," Rosso said, determined to change the subject. "Since when do you speak Yiddish?"

"Since I'm dating a Jew."

Rosso glanced at his mother, then examined his dessert plate. He stared for a full minute at the chocolate covering his spoon. "You're *dating?*" he asked.

"Yes."

"And he's Jewish?"

"Yes."

Rosso looked up and stared at his mother. "They say they make good husbands," he said mechanically.

"I don't *need* a husband!" his mother exclaimed. "But after thirty years," she said, leaning towards Rosso, "I need a companion."

"I'm happy for you," Rosso said, wishing he could summon up more joy. "Just shocked. That's all."

Rosso told himself it would take time to adjust to this momentous development. His own mother, after raising two children alone, had found someone with whom to walk, play bridge, and share her life. Rosso had always pictured his father as that person. In his mind, Mother and Father were always together, always laughing, and forever young. His father had died at thirty-nine—Rosso's age on his next birthday. Now, thirty years later, Rosso realized that he had not accepted his father's death. Or rather, he had, but only conditionally. Because until now, no one had dared to take his place.

Rosso sat in a daze. This was not what he had expected to hear over lunch the day he happened to be flying into Newark.

"His name is Gus," his mother said. "He's financially secure, a good dancer, and a real gentleman."

"How old?"

"Seventy-five."

As Rosso paid the bill, Flora went on to say that she was the envy of her widows group, since Gus was one of the very few seniors who could drive at night.

The more Flora talked, the more Rosso realized that his mother had been seeing Gus for months. They had even discussed moving in together. She admitted that her outburst over Maria had nothing to do with his date. Or, as his mother explained, it did and it didn't.

"I'm so *worried* about you," she said.

Rosso told his mother that it was a difficult time, but that he would get through it.

Flora explained that it was impossible for her to be happy when her own son was sad.

"I'm not sad," Rosso insisted.

"Yes, you are!" his mother cried. "And you *need* someone."

A few minutes later, after Rosso promised to smear aloe on his lip, Flora appeared calmer.

"You might have to keep your conversations with Dad to a minimum," Rosso said, forcing a smile. "Gus probably doesn't believe in the afterlife."

"Do you? his mother asked, with an intensity that took Rosso by surprise.

"I was baptized. I received Holy Communion and was confirmed in fifth grade."

"You had to believe then. What do you believe now?"

"That I'll see my father again," Rosso said.

With this, his mother started to cry. Not because she had lost her husband, but because her son had lost his father.

The answer to the question that Maria had put to Rosso, however crudely, was this: The loss of his father had changed him in a manner any child acquainted with grief would understand. There was no single thing he could point to. Rather, he possessed a perspective—a general sense of life being random, fragile, and finite.

In practical matters, it meant that he often wanted to intervene when he saw anyone arguing with a loved one. He wanted to tell them to be grateful for all the moments they took for granted—however marred, sentimental, or disappointing. To all the sons, especially, he wanted to tell them to be thankful that there exists a man who will drive you to the ski bus at 5 a.m.; who will take vacation days to look at colleges with you; who will root for you during even your most lackluster hockey game; who will brag about you until your ears burn; and who will help you make sense of your life.

In personal matters, it meant that for years, Rosso had invested *The Spirit of St. Louis* with more significance than it probably held, as if the text encoded a message about the father he would never know. When Rosso had been old enough to read Lindbergh's memoir himself, he did so over and over again and decided that his father, like him, had always secretly wanted to fly.

Finally, the death of Rosso's father made him realize that he had been drawn to Charles for a reason. Every day, his friend grappled with the one thing no one wanted to talk about. Charles was the only one of his friends who was intimate with death.

A few weeks after Charles had finished his surgical training, Rosso made a series of changes in his life which, however modest, made him feel significant. He put a bumper sticker on his car—the same one Charles had: *Don't take your organs to heaven. Heaven knows we need them here.* At the post office, he turned in his Old Glories for the "Share a Life" stamps. Finally, quietly, and without fanfare, he checked the "Organ Donor" box when his license came up for renewal.

6

---

Every six months, Rosso took a couple of days off and drove to Danbury to see his sister, Elaine. During these visits, he would watch his favorite Bugs Bunny episodes with his nephews, then scan the listings for Mister Ed.

During his last visit, Elaine had reminded him that his fifteenth college reunion was coming up. "You never know," she said. So Rosso went to Hanover—*not* because he was looking for love. Rather, he wanted to revisit a time in his life, which, in hindsight, felt less com- plicated.

Hours into the reunion dinner, Rosso learned what his friends were doing with their lives. Thanks to an exceptionally healthy bond market, the class of '83's resident expert on Kafka had retired at thirty. The class philosopher was now the editor of an internet fund magazine. The class poet was booking guests for Rosie O'Donnell. And one of Rosso's hockey buddies had made a fortune importing oil when the Soviet Union was on its knees.

Then they asked about Rosso. His software consulting business was booming, he said. But why, they wondered, had he shown up without his wife? When Rosso mentioned that he was in the final stages of divorce, they were sympathetic. Yet it was not long before these well-meant condolences took the form of an open season on Doris. Nobody understood what Rosso had seen in her.

Simplistic and idiotic as it sounded, Doris during her Hampshire College years had been an original. Quirky, kind, and funny without trying to be, Doris had the added virtue of being one of the few women he knew who wasn't interviewing for a bank. Not that Rosso had anything against banking. What he objected to was the collective failure of imagination on campus. So, when Irving Trust, Bankers Trust, European-American, Manufacturers Hanover, and Morgan Guaranty were siphoning the brains of his entire generation, what was Doris doing? Painting cherubs on the inside of a clavichord.

From the class of '83, Rosso could count the people he admired on one hand: poor, sweet, Iris, the class's only social worker; Teddy Klein, a primary caregiver for adults with Downs Syndrome; Thomas "Kafka" Elkin, who had donated thirty percent of his considerable fortune to the Cystic Fibrosis Foundation. And Charles Dine, his maddingly complex friend, who had been on call the weekend of the reunion.

Rosso emerged from his reunion with a certainty about two things. First, he knew why he had married Doris, though it would take considerably more time to figure out why his marriage had failed. Second (and on a vastly more superficial note), he learned that he would have to remarry before he lost his hair—because at the reunion, Rosso had witnessed the demise of Ernesto "Matadór" Bravo, Dartmouth's greatest living lover.

As a freshman, Matadór had seduced the school's only virgin in the laundry room. As a sophomore, he had serenaded an adjunct professor out of the arms of her husband. And as a junior, he had married "Miss Rainforest, 1982," the heiress to a Brazilian cocoa fortune. Yet, at the reunion, it had taken Rosso a full hour to identify the small, thin man by the punchbowl. Ernesto's tousled black hair, velvet eyelashes, and flamenco guitar playing had given way to eyes dull as pearl onions and a buffed head, bald as a pool hall cue.

On the second day of his visit, Elaine made Rosso hold the boys for shots—a task which, in emotional difficulty, he found second only to putting his beloved Lab from childhood, Brandy, to sleep. Elaine would leave the room. Dr. Paige would ready her needle and say to each child, "I don't like this any more than you do." Then Rosso would do his best to calm the screaming that followed. After he had succeeded in consoling one of his three nephews, the door would open a crack and Elaine would push another one in, eyes frozen with fear.

The visits to Dr. Paige were equally stressful for Elaine. The last one had gone like this.

"Brian's holding his own bottle!"
"He should be on the sippy cup."
"He's crawling."
"He should be walking."
"He's feeding himself."
"He should be using a fork. Does he wave hello?"
"No."
"Any words? "
"No."
"How about hi? Hi, Brian,'" Dr. Paige coaxed.

No reaction. Brian would be silent, huge, and philosophical, then, all of a sudden, he'd let out a giant EEE!

That night after dinner, Rosso told the G-rated version of his X-rated encounter with Michelle. After the children had gone to bed, Rosso tried to learn more about this parochial school vixen.

"She didn't act married," Rosso said.

"What do you mean?" Elaine eyed Rosso with irritation. She confessed that she had lost touch with Michelle but issued the stock response of a strict Catholic who had no patience for adulterous slander. "You don't know her," she said abruptly.

Fine. I don't know her, Rosso thought. I played golf with her husband. I made love to Our Lady of the Ocean Club, a so-called happily married Catholic. But, clearly, I don't know her.

Rosso wanted to pursue the matter, but something stopped him, as it always did with Elaine. In part, because his sister was always *doing* something. He'd had conversations about flying with her dishwasher on the scrub cycle; debates over divorce while the *Dirt Devil* sucked up broken glass; and ruminations about his nephews' futures with her breast pump whirring.

Elaine asked about the women he was dating. When none of them appealed to her, Rosso changed the subject, thinking his sister would have *something* to say about their mother's boyfriend. "Have you met Gus?" he asked.

"Sure," she said matter-of-factly. "They're very cute together." Elaine cleared the children's tableware, sippy cups, tray tables, and plates. When the phone rang, she picked it up and started assembling a plate of food for her husband, Carl, who called to say that he was on his way home. After she had hung up, Elaine covered the plate with plastic wrap and said, "Mom didn't want to upset you." Then she turned away and flipped the switch to the disposal.

The grinding sound stripped Rosso's nerves. "Do you have to do that *now*?" he shouted.

Elaine didn't hear him.

Rosso stared at his sister's thick, wavy, tobacco-brown hair, her large soulful eyes, and tried to imagine the last time he had seen her beautiful, bright smile. Despite their uncanny resemblance, Rosso could not believe they came from the same family.

After Elaine had finished with the disposal, she slid a sponge out of her Price Club jumbo pack, smeared it with anti-bacterial soap, and said, "I don't dwell on things the way you do. Gus seems like a good man. Mom looks happy." Then she started scouring the sink.

The conversation didn't go any deeper because Elaine didn't go any deeper. The problem was that, right now, Rosso needed *someone* to fathom his all-too-human condition. Maybe his mother was right. Maybe he was sad. Maybe he *was* in crisis. Maybe he needed a little more than the usual *very nice day, ho-hum so what; other than that, Mrs. Lincoln, how did you like the play?*

After all these years, Rosso realized that he had *no idea* what went on in his sister's mind. Rosso loved her, but, though he would never say it, he found Elaine so goddamned boring. She was a good mother, yes. But a real snooze. Drink your milk, eat your broccoli, try the tofu. He had never *once* heard Elaine belt out a tune. No "Itsy-Bitsy Spider," no "Old MacDonald," no "Zip-a-Dee-Doo-Dah."

Yet, what if Elaine was the perfect example of what marriage and young children were about?

The idea that all women might end up like Elaine triggered some Strangelovian anti-dating reflex in Rosso. From the depths of his already chronic reluctance to take the whole process of dating seriously, Rosso summoned up the image of Rita. Rita, too, was exhausted. Rita had zinc salve under her nails from two kids in diapers. Rita took care of her kids (and worked part-time). The difference was that Rita had energy, humor, and, even in her darkest moments, always managed either to hum a few bars to her children or sing outright.

When Carl arrived home, Elaine dropped a plate of reheated meatloaf in front of him. His tired eyes, shrunken behind thick, foggy glasses, brightened when he saw Rosso.

He kissed his wife, removed his coat, and sat down for

dinner. "Your mother's got a fella," he said sweetly. "She's doing better than any of us."

Rosso laughed. Flora *was* doing well. And he had always appreciated Carl's keen eye for the absurd. Carl Thorne was a lazy, brilliant man who did what all men of his kind do—he taught high school math. The fact that he was brilliant only made him more unhappy and self-aware than his colleagues. As for Elaine, she did what the wives of all brilliant, lazy men do—she harangued her husband for his sloth, his overeating, and read biographies of Rose Kennedy in an effort to turn her sons into the kind of men she could both love and respect.

"That shirt doesn't fit," Elaine said, shoving a bowl of green beans towards him.

Rosso braced himself for the kind of scene all single people endure when married couples share entirely too much of their private life with a guest.

"Leave him alone," Rosso said. He looked at Carl, whose shirt was tight as the skin on a frankfurter. Yet, thanks to Carl's gentle presence, Rosso was experiencing a conversion. He found himself wanting to like Gus, wanting to like any man who made his mother happy—who made her feel alive. As long as Rosso didn't find his mother riffling through a dog-eared copy of the *Victoria's Secret* catalogue, he could live with Gus.

As for Carl, he had learned to ignore Elaine. Sensing the atmospheric imbalance, he resorted to the trustworthiness of his compulsions. He began clearing the plate of food in front of him. Elaine observed the bored look on Carl's face as he followed one forkful of meatloaf with another. She had once told Rosso, "Large people eat that way—slowly, mechanically, as if they could not *possibly* manage another bite. To Rosso, the poor man looked lonely —as if food were his only solace and his plate a friendly port of call in an otherwise troubled day.

Rosso settled into the basement. Elaine had left him sheets with Dumbo on them, along with a blanket the color and texture of corrugated cardboard. He glanced at the queen-size sofabed and began tossing the frilly needlepoint pillows onto the floor. Eight in total. *Ridiculous*, he muttered to himself. He pulled the metal bar, but it refused to yield the mattress. When it finally did, the force of his unresisted yank whacked his back against the doorknob to the laundry room, which contained a smelly oil burner.

Rosso decided that, at thirty-eight, he was tired of being a guest. Actually, it was more mean-spirited than that; he was tired of staying in small rooms with tiny sofabeds that you have to make yourself. The shitty ventilation was no less consoling. One of his tennis heroes had died of carbon monoxide poisoning while staying in a guest room above a pool.

Rosso made the bed, then signed on. He was determined to apologize to the French woman he had offended and to chat with both the Belle of Amherst and the freelance writer from Boston who allegedly looked like the young Elizabeth Taylor.

In part, he needed an antidote to the concentration of domesticity he was witnessing at his sister's house. Elaine and Carl made him and Doris look like newlyweds. Which raised a disturbing question. Why *had* he and Doris divorced?

Other than golf, Labs, and Rosso's desire for children, their worst arguments had been about grocery shopping. Doris had reproached him for his inattention to detail. She would send him out for Thomas English Muffins and he returned with Pepperidge Farm. If the deli line was more than six tickets long, fresh cold cuts came back vacuum-packed. Grated Romano came back as Parmesan and Dannon yogurt, when it came back at all, was in huge tubs where, Doris insisted, if you scooped out a tablespoon, a brackish puddle of yellow liquid filled the hole.

At first, Rosso attributed his wife's pickiness to the fact that she was an artist and possessed a superior aesthetic, but as time passed, he wondered if she was not simply a pain in the ass.

As for Doris, she accused Rosso of purposely defying her.

"Everything I ask for always comes back the opposite of what I want—so basically you're ignoring me," she would say. "You're saying you can't be bothered making me happy."

Rosso would reply that there was nothing deliberate about his actions. What's more, since he cared very little what brand of yogurt he ate, it was hard for him to understand what, from his perspective, seemed like a constant series of overreactions provoked by his well-meaning visits to the grocery store.

All this would arouse Doris's fury, because she claimed that Rosso was *very* particular about things *he* cared about. And even if *she* herself did *not* care, she went *out of her way* to *respect* his demands.

"Like when?" he once asked.

"If you want coffee ice cream, it has to be Starbucks. And not just *any* Starbucks ice cream, but Starbucks Italian Roast ice cream—*not* Java Chip and *not* Dark Espresso Swirl!"

Doris claimed that she often ended up going to four different stores to get it.

Rosso had to admit that what Doris said was true.

But had all this constituted grounds for divorce? Especially since, for Doris's sake, he had *changed*—a task which, in daily effort, rivaled the labor of Sisyphus. What came naturally to Doris did not occur in nature for Rosso. So really, he wondered, shouldn't the person *doing* the changing, as opposed to the so-called "perfect" person dishing out the criticism, get more credit? Instead, on February 13, 1997, just when Rosso had begun to execute his wife's grocery list with the cheerful precision of a professional shopper, Doris served him papers.

All this made Rosso feel lonely—so lonely that he felt like buying a quart of scotch and drinking himself blotto. Instead, he did something he had never done. In his sister's basement, he spent a couple of hours in chat rooms, playing amorous roulette on the Net. For the first time, he even opened some of the spam e-mail he routinely deleted.

"Like big tits?" "Want to suck and fuck?" "TEEN SEX!" and "Ever seen one of these!?"—with before and after pictures of a penis enhanced *Two Inches!* by a Guaranteed Penis-Extender *for just $19.95*! This pornographic excrement floating through cyberspace, Rosso decided, was not at all titillating. If anything, it left him feeling even more desolate.

Rosso called up the November list. Only three entries for the tri-state area. Unless the Smartheart proved compellingly travel worthy, he had decided not to cast his net as far as he had for Elizabeth Taylor.

**Smartheart, Inc. November Listing.**
Portfolio Manager (32). Civic-minded Georgetown graduate who believes you are what you do (New York).

Georgetown wasn't an Ivy, so Rosso's first reaction was to wonder who at Smartheart was minding the gate. Since Rosso knew some outstanding Georgetown graduates, he downloaded her bio.

**Smartheart Inc.**

**Name:** Elizabeth Dyson

**Occupation** : Portfolio Manager

**Schools:** Georgetown; B.A. in Philosophy

**Address:** 22 Springlake, Larchmont, New York

**Age:** 32. **Height:** 5'11

**Description:** Blonde Hair, Blue Eyes

FABIENNE MARSH

**Status:** Single

**Children:** None

**Religion:** Catholic

**Hobbies (in order of importance):** Volunteer work and tennis.

**Favorite Books:** *The Bridges of Madison County*.

**What are you looking for in a companion?** A devout Christian who wants to raise a family.

Tall glass of water, but too Junior League for him. Worse still was her literary vacuity. Next!

**Smartheart, Inc. November Listing.**
Medical Librarian (38) who doesn't look like one. Barnard Graduate who loves animals and nature (New York).

Rosso took a look at her bio.

**Smartheart Inc.**

**Name:** Mina Purna

**Occupation:** Medical Librarian, Mount Sinai Hospital

**Schools:** Barnard; B.A. in English.

**Address:** 502 Rochambeau Drive, White Plains, New York

**Age:** 31. **Height:** 5'4

**Description:** Dark hair, dark eyes

**Status:** Single

**Children:** None

**Religion:** Hindu

**Hobbies (in order of importance):** UNICEF, Health Club and *The Sound of Music* (I have seen it twelve times)

**Favorite Books:** *The Wizard of Oz* and *Doctor Doolitle*

**What are you looking for in a companion?** A culturally sensitive man who honors his own traditions and respects those of others.

Wow. Childlike, Rosso observed. Probably shares an apartment with her mother in Westchester. After Doris had dumped him in the winter of '81, Rosso had dated a brilliant and fascinating Indian woman named Anna, who had been born an Untouchable. Rosso had spent the first few dates trying to convince Anna that, in America, immigrants are welcome. When she failed to believe him, he had decided that some cultural boundaries were better left intact.

**Smartheart, Inc. November Listing.**
Museum Curator (35). Princeton graduate seeks confident man with good sense of humor to ski, scale mountains, and explore life's outer and innermost landscapes (New York City).

Rosso could not sense her, so he called up the bio.

**Smartheart Inc.**

**Name:** Jacqueline Susann

**Occupation:** Museum Curator

**Schools:** Princeton; B.A. in Art History

**Address:** 322 East 95th Street, New York City

**Age:** 35. **Height:** 5'8"

**Description:** Brown hair; brown eyes (picture on file)

**Status:** Single

**Children:** None

**Religion:** Baptist

**Hobbies (in order of importance):** Museum going, reading, outdoor sports, and choral works.

**Favorite Books:** *One Hundred Years of Solitude* and *Their Eyes Were Watching God* by Zora Neale Hurston.

**What are you looking for in a companion?** A man with humor, refinement, and superior values.

"Picture on file" was pretty rare. Rosso beat himself up for a minute, telling himself that he should not care what Jacqueline looked like. Her picture, he assumed, was a pre-emptive strike—her way of saying "if you want an interesting woman, don't expect a beauty too." To Rosso's surprise, the picture he downloaded was of a stunning woman with a warm smile and expressive brown eyes. She also happened to be black.

Rosso's first thought was that his mother would kill him. His second was even more formidable. What if Jacqueline only dated men of color? Impossible, he determined. You can't survive romantically at Princeton if you only date men of color. All those scrawny tow-headed trustfunders. She needed a real man, Rosso decided. A Dartmouth man. Still, he could not be sure. He drafted a note.

> *I was intrigued by your bio and your winsome photograph. Forgive me for being blunt, but there is no other way: Do you date (tall, dark, handsome) white. Men of Italian-American descent?*

Rosso had just sent Jacqueline's e-mail when he heard a knock. He glanced at the clock—10:15—and opened the door. Carl stood in his pajamas, holding five catalogues with Post-its marking various pages.

"Elaine says I need a new wardrobe," he said.

Poor bastard, Rosso thought. For the next half hour, he and Carl circled five items and made out the order forms. Carl put stamps on the envelopes and left them under Elaine's pillow.

Rosso flipped off the light and turned to the Classic Sports channel. He relived the anguish he had felt in 1986 when the Red Sox lost the World Series. The only difference now was that his grief was compounded by the fact that one of the guys on the bench was Doris's boyfriend. He reached for his laptop and was about to turn it off when the long-awaited "Elizabeth Taylor" appeared online.

Her wisdom and humor came to be something Rosso craved at his loneliest hours.

Liz: Hello.
JR: Hi. I'm Jim. I ordered your bio. You've caught me by surprise. Watching a ball game, actually.
Liz: Sorry.
JR: Don't be. When men are losing ground, they need to talk about sports. It's a male homing device.
Liz: Why are you losing ground?
JR: For a number of reasons I don't know you well enough to talk about.
Liz: Fine. But if a man's team loses a game—to a man, it's worse than any amorous calamity.
JR: It's a different kind of love lost.
Liz: But to a man an equivalent pain.
JR: Possibly.
Liz: Mets fans harbor one of the greatest loves.
JR: Yes, they do!
Liz: But the purest love has to be that of the Red Sox fan.
JR: Why?
Liz: Because it's unconsummated.
JR: That's what I used to think.
Liz: Everybody knows that the Red Sox never put out. They haven't won a World Series since World War I.
JR: Let's change the subject.
Liz: I upset you.
JR: My ex-wife's consorting with a Red Sock.
Liz: I had no idea.
JR: What does it take for a woman to do what she did?
Liz: Leave you?
JR: What does it take for anyone to go beyond their thoughts and fantasies destabilizing their entire life for love?
Liz: A lot.
JR: Why?
Liz: It's not safe.

JR: Not safe because?
Liz: Human wreckage is a pretty stiff consequence.
JR: If that were true, then men and women wouldn't have as many affairs as they do.
Liz: Affairs don't interest me.
JR: Why not?
Liz: They satisfy an itch.
JR: People have been scratching that so-called itch since time began!
Liz: People have been satisfying all kinds of instincts since time began.
JR: But to have an affair, there's some feeling involved.
Liz: Of course. But not love, necessarily. Some of the best physical encounters would fail if emotions were introduced.
JR: What if the itch doesn't go away?
Liz: Then it's not an itch.
JR: What is it?
Liz: A yearning. A hunger. A conflict. More than skin deep.
JR: That's what I have.
Liz: When you love someone you don't stop desiring other people, you just don't act on it.
JR: Because it would be wrong?
Liz: No. Because you would hurt them.

Rosso's session was interrupted. To his frustration, all he had was an e-mail address for "Liz."

He revisited the September listings to see if they held a clue. Not only was there no trace of this captivating Smartheart from Boston, but the rest of September's listings were a wash. He had been right about the Vassar MD. She was an emergency room doctor for a large HMO because, she explained, "There's minimal patient contact and it pays well." So go buy yourself a

Lancelot, Rosso thought. As for the Woman who allegedly Ran With Wolves, she wouldn't have recognized the animal if it had stared out of her television on a *National Geographic* Special.

Rosso was so intrigued by Liz Taylor's aura that he had trouble falling asleep. He checked his e-mail. Nothing from Liz. Since she had sent an instant message, after which they had met in one of Smartheart's private chatrooms, it was entirely possible that she had not even ordered his bio. That meant that Liz had no way of contacting him, except if they happened to be online at the same time.

Before going to bed, Rosso responded to Phoebe's steady trail of sylphlike e-notes by agreeing to meet her for dinner. After that, he composed an e-mail to the French woman he had offended and scanned the real estate listings for apartments cheap enough to reduce his overhead. He toyed with the idea of selling his house. The memories of life with Doris were too keen.

# 7

Rosso pulled into his driveway and saw a basket with a bow on it. There were so many new people in his life, he honestly had no idea who might have sent it. Mrs. Becker was always a possibility. She had once left a bottle of champagne on his doorstep with a card reading, "Let me sell this house and you'll be taking bubble baths in Dom Perignon!"

But this time there was no note, only a basket. Inside was a puppy. A Labrador.

Rosso did not notice the brown suede shoes, both sensible and fetching, walking towards him.

"Do you like her?" Doris asked.

He looked up. Rosso's love of puppies and Doris's impromptu visit rendered him speechless. He cradled the Lab. The puppy licked his finger. Agony. "I've got to go," Rosso said, not too convincingly. He fumbled for the car keys in his pocket, dropped them, then retrieved them. "Besides, I work full time. It wouldn't be fair to him."

"She's a girl, " Doris said quietly.

"You had a baby girl! " Rosso whispered, his voice strangled with emotion.

"No. The puppy. She's a girl."

Doris sat on the steps next to Rosso. "How are you?"

"Okay. Not great. How about you?" he asked.

He had not seen Doris in months and already she looked more sophisticated. She wore a mulch-brown mini skirt with a touchably thick, pink Angora turtleneck—a far cry from her long skirt and hiking boot days. Her glossy brown hair was swept back in a French twist, revealing her sensuous profile.

She turned to look at him. "Didn't you get my email?"

"No." Rosso steeled himself against a reply he expected would include a paean for her Red Sox, a rhapsody on maternity, and an *andante con brillo* regarding her newfound happiness.

"I had a miscarriage," she said. "So, for now," she continued, with remarkable evenness and strength, "I'll take care of Rascal."

Rosso was dumbfounded. He felt Doris remove the puppy from his arms. She'd had a miscarriage. The puppy was for *her*. It was too much to process.

"I'm sorry," he said.

They sat in silence, watching the sun dance on Rascal's glossy coat. Rosso sensed that Doris was waiting for him to pose the question she desperately wanted to answer.

"What are you doing here?" he asked. Rosso was curious.

"I wanted you to meet Rascal," she said, stroking the dog. "I wonder if I might drop her off sometimes. I promise not to overdo it."

Rosso tried not to look at the puppy. Any creature with four legs and a tail had always been welcome in his house. "All right," he said. "But make sure you find some backup in case I'm out of town."

"I will," Doris said. "You're the only one I trust," she smiled. She gently placed Rascal in the basket and thanked Rosso for the visit.

Halfway to her car, she turned back. "I miss you," she said.

That night, Rosso lay awake, wishing the puppy had been for him. I miss you, Doris had said. You can't say that to a man you divorced twenty-three months before, a man who missed her but who knew, as Doris did, that they were past the point of reconciliation.

Rosso wondered if their move to the suburbs had precipitated the crisis. He had hoped they would start a family, that Doris would become the mother of his children. Instead, at the age of thirty-four, she told him she was losing her identity. It had been easier to be a lemming in New York City, carried along in a school of equally confused people, than it was to stand apart in the suburbs. Not quite a wife, not yet a mother, not fully a professional—just a sweet, rudderless girl with no sense of herself other than what was reflected back at her by those who nonetheless loved her.

At seven o'clock the following evening, Rosso sat in the harsh light of the squash court waiting for Charles. He was often late and his beeper sometimes called him away in the middle of a game.

That said, Charles was worth the wait. He was a disciplined athlete who knew which shots to play and when to play them. Rosso was hurled all over the court—diving for the ball, slamming against the wall—as though he was waging war against a tornado. Charles often won, without moving off the "T."

This gift for strategy made Charles, who felt at home in the stodgiest country club, a good tennis player and a superb golfer. As for Rosso, his determination, strength, and quick reflexes made him excel at hockey and rugby.

When the glass door opened, to Rosso's surprise, Charles appeared on time in his favorite t-shirt, the one with Snoopy in scrubs.

"I can't believe you still wear that thing, " Rosso said.

"Rita bought it for me."

"It's too small."

"I like it," Charles said. He stretched the fabric over his sleeve, as if making room for enormous biceps. "Stand up and prepare to be annihilated." He hit the ball against the wall with considerable force.

Rosso lost the first game on a tie-breaker, was beaten soundly on the second, and, as predicted, was annihilated on the third. They sat down for a break.

"What's the matter?" Charles asked.

"What do you mean?"

"Snoops and I aren't even breaking a sweat."

"Sorry."

"You haven't played this badly since February of '81."

"The night Doris dumped me," Rosso said.

He remembered what a good friend Charles had been that winter. Rosso had moaned, "How could she dump me for *him!?*"

Charles had glanced at the offender's cropped hair, goatee, pierced ear, and motorcycle jacket and uttered, "He's obviously a thespian," dwelling on the 's' to make it hiss.

"They have power over women," Rosso had said. "I can't figure it out."

"Young women who feel unfinished think a male artist can turn them into a masterpiece."

For Rosso, with apparent effortlessness, Charles had solved one of the great mysteries regarding women's taste in men.

Rosso grabbed his racquet and stood up. "Score?"

"Three zip."

"But who's counting?" Rosso laughed.

"Any Smartheart prospects?" Charles asked, suddenly indifferent to defending his title.

Rosso took one hard look at his friend, as if to gauge just how much ridicule was likely to drip off Charles onto him.

"Phoebe's on the calendar," he said, examining the strings on his racquet.

"The kinky California girl?"

"Yeah."

"Wasn't there another one?"

"Elizabeth Taylor."

"Is that her name!?"

"No."

"What's her real name?"

"I don't know."

"Have you met her?"

"No."

"Have you spoken with her?"

"Online."

"But you're stuck on her."

"Yes," Rosso said, bouncing the racquet off his palm. "I can't explain it. We connect."

Charles looked at Rosso as if he were about to request a psychiatric consult.

"What are you looking at?" Rosso asked.

"I have a feeling that you're not finished."

"I'm not."

"Who else?"

"You know her."

"Yes, but do *you*?"

"Of course I do! I was married to her."

"Oh, Jesus! Not the typesetter—"

"Bookbinder, goddamnit! How many times do I have to tell you?"

Charles apologized as a courtesy to his friend, but privately he dismissed the idea of Rosso's return to Doris. They were divorced, after all, which, in human affairs, is as surgical as it gets.

"Sometimes I think you need a dog," Charles said, politely changing the subject to something he also believed to be true.

"I almost got one," Rosso said brightly. He spotted two women at the door to the squash court and waved them in.

During dinner, Charles's beeper went off. Since the restaurant was empty, he used his cell phone to call the transplant coordinator.

"Un huh. Yeah. What's the patient's name? Thanks." Then Charles hung up.

"I can do that, Rosso said, mimicking a few of the conversations he had overheard over the years. His favorite being "Is it bilious or bloody?"

Charles smiled.

"Do you want to cancel our order?" Rosso asked.

"No. The harvest will take six hours. The labs, a couple more. If the liver's any good, the case won't go until 3 a.m." He looked at his watch. "I'd better call Rita."

People had started arriving, so Charles retired to the foyer to call his wife. Rosso sat there nursing his beer. He had wanted to tell Charles about Doris's miscarriage but decided against it. He was tired of rushing through intimate revelations or having them interrupted by a beeper. Besides, Charles would dismiss Rosso's confusion entirely and focus on the fact that Doris hadn't even married the guy.

The waitress arrived with a plate of fried calamari. "Want a refill?" she asked, pointing to Rosso's beer.

"No thanks," he said, handing her the empty bottle.

Rosso stared at the calimari. Charles was the only man who, when answering his pages, made Rosso feel like a wife. A wife who had married badly. He wondered why mothers, generation after generation, advised their daughters to marry doctors. Dentists, yes. Internists, maybe. But surgeons, *especially* transplant surgeons—the very suggestion that doctors made good husbands was enough to call the mother-daughter bond into question.

Charles returned to the table and apologized for having to cut their meal short. "I've got one hour," he said. "I want to see my kids before they go to bed."

When the check arrived, Rosso and Charles sparred over whose turn it was to pay. Charles insisted it was his, as he always did. He had never forgotten Rosso's generosity during his training. M.D.; Ph.D.; five years as a general surgery resident; one year of vascular surgery; two more years as a transplant fellow. Fourteen years total. Until three years ago, when Charles had become a staff physician at St. John's, he had never held a job that paid more than thirty-five thousand a year. The best surgeons who, like Charles, affiliated themselves with teaching hospitals made a fraction the salary of their counterparts in private practice. The trade-off was that their cases were far more interesting. "He'd be bored doing gall bladders all day," Rita always said. Now that Charles was an overworked and esteemed member of St. John's faculty, he was making ninety-six thousand dollars a year.

"Your salary's pathetic," Rosso said, determined, this time, to provoke Charles out of paying the bill.

8

In Rita's house is a room in which, with the exception of Charles, no one goes. Charles called it his study in the basement, but it was more than that because he descended only when he was spent and emerged restored in some way that eluded explanation.

One night, last August, Rita went in. She had put the children to bed and sought a place to work. After Labor Day, she had become a part-time employee of Smartheart. The job was not what Rita's degree in European history had prepared her for, nor would she put it on her resumé. For a mother, it was good part-time work. The idea was to make enough money so that Charles would not have to supplement their income by taking trauma call.

At a children's playgroup, Rita had met Louise Jeffry, a young grandmother and Smartheart co-founder who had offered her the job. Louise had hired Rita because she was concerned that Smartheart's screening techniques were unsophisticated. She also needed help recruiting new members through word of mouth. Since Rita had been a charter member of Smartheart, Louise was relieved to hire someone familiar with her organization.

Beyond Rita's need to work and Louise's need for help, they had little in common. Louise, who was fifty-five, had written articles about raising non-sexist children, growing health food gardens at home, and controlling her orgasms. Most of her girlfriends were well-educated and had espoused feminism, investing it with an ideological rigor, which, in hindsight, they found it did not possess. They had never lied about their ages, nor had they ever colored their hair.

Yet, for all their militance, they had married, had babies, and, until their children were in high school, had never gone to work. Many of their husbands were now divorcing them and, in the case of Louise's husband, dating younger women.

Rita was urged to keep a list of all the men and women she knew who were single. Her duties were to collect documents proving that her candidates had gone to Ivy League schools. Then she was to help them write a short bio, which would appear on the monthly list. The longer one was up to them after Louise had reviewed their credentials.

Two hundred dollars for every new Ivy League subscriber was Rita's commission, but only if she met her quota—five people a month. The month before, her first, she had been successful. Rita was by no means Louise's only source for candidates. Seventy-five percent of Smartheart's eight thousand members had responded to ads in their respective alumni magazines.

Rita carefully recorded each new phone number, address, and name. Four in total, just below quota. She drummed her fingers on the desk and noticed a small cherrywood file with a latch on it. Since Charles kept his checkbook, his tax returns, and all his personal papers casually within reach, Rita found this island of privacy odd. She made a few calls and, while reaching for a pencil, noticed a small key in the top drawer of the desk.

Rita had always been respectful of Charles's or anyone else's privacy, but it was tantalizing to have the key to the only secret her husband seemed to possess. To take her mind off the file, she wrote up her first month's candidates—a male first amendment lawyer she had literally bumped into while swimming at the YMCA; a female National Park ranger from Montana (friend of a friend); a divorced mother of two she had met at the pharmacy while waiting for her daughter's antibiotic; and a young teacher who taught at the local elementary school (her neighbor's daughter).

Her eyes wandered back to the file. She wondered if the key in the drawer was the right one and a pinch of fear took hold the moment she imagined testing it.

Twenty minutes later, Rita forced the key slightly which, in turn, opened the lock. She lifted the file's small lid and there, very neatly organized, were the names of patients Charles had operated on over the years.

Psychiatrists often kept elaborate notes on their patients, but this was rare for surgeons. So it was with some surprise that Rita began to examine what looked like the home version of her husband's more elaborate hospital charts. On closer inspection, the cards before her revealed how devoted her husband was both to his profession and to his patients. "Terrible suffering" she read of one patient whose leg Charles, as a resident, eventually had to amputate. "Courageous " he had written, next to the medical history of a young man with recurrent parathyroid cancer. "Inspiring" he had noted, next to the name of a famous ballplayer who had received a new liver. Finally, on the card for a little girl whose cancer had been detected too late, Charles had written "Inoperable."

Towards the back, a series of cards had commanded an uncommonly large portion of Charles's attention.

***Anne Farrell. 35.***
*Referral from Brigham.*
*Acute pancreatitis.*
*Discharged after forty-five days.*
*Returned with complications.*

She fingered the next card. Still Anne Farrell. The notes grew more personal and Charles, who had kept a maximum of two cards for each patient, had reserved six for Anne.

Rita was deeply moved by the notes, but as she read more carefully, their intimacy began to make her uncomfortable. Compared with the already comprehensive notes she had read, Charles's entries for Anne seemed excessive. What's more, behind the cards was a tiny, brown paper bag. On its surface, in red marker, was an image that took her breath away—that of a perfectly drawn heart.

Just then, Rita heard Charles's relaxed gait on the floor above. She tucked the bag behind the cards and slammed the file shut. Then she locked the box and put the key back in the drawer.

Upstairs, Charles was all smiles. The Whipple, a long and difficult operation for pancreatic cancer, had gone smoothly.

"But eventually the patient will die?" Rita asked.

"Yes," Charles said, his smile eclipsed. "But five years is a long time for someone who expected to be dead within a week."

"Do you have to go back in?" she asked.

"There's an emergency."

There was always an emergency. Charles would come home for an hour, have dinner, and return to the hospital.

He pointed upstairs, looking hopeful, to where the children slept. "Did I miss them?"

"By an hour," Rita said.

He offered to make dinner, and when he asked Rita why she looked so glum, she simply said that she missed him.

"I'm the luckiest man in the world," he said, kissing Rita. He grabbed her hand, pulled her upstairs into Tina's room, and smiled on seeing the empty bottle she had hurled onto the floor. In the neighboring room, Daniel had fallen asleep with a stuffed dog in one hand and a dump truck in the other.

After Charles left, Rita returned to the basement. She stared at the form for her Smartheart candidates. Then she looked at Charles's file and forbade herself to open it.

Once she had booted up her old laptop, she started typing in what she had for Louise. She stared at the four names, then, on a lark, found herself typing in the name Anne Farrell. She added an e-mail address, insisting to Louise that Anne didn't wish any other information revealed about her, and dashed off Anne's short bio, which she sent along with the rest of her September candidates.

**Smartheart, Inc. September Listing.**
Freelance writer (34). Young Elizabeth Taylor look-alike seeks boxer-poet. Intense, yet soft spot for Elvis. (Boston).

## 9

When Rosso failed to catch "Elizabeth Taylor" online, he redirected his energy into less healthy pursuits. He started working like a fiend and dating in a manner which, for a man who had been celibate between Doris and Michelle, was downright promiscuous.

The dates, both setups from well-meaning neighbors and Smartheart Ivies, followed the course of a predictable train wreck: dinner followed by drinks at a fancy bar. By 11 p.m., she'd asked him up. By 11:30, she'd told him her mother gave her G.I. Joe when she had wanted Barbie. By midnight, Rosso had recovered his first and only suppressed memory, announcing that his father had never taken him to Disneyland. At 1 a.m., she'd admit she wasn't over some jerk, then pinned a confused Rosso against her bed. Whether they had sex or not, the truth without exception was that by 3 a.m., it was crybaby time. Daddy left mommy, mommy left daddy, Uncle Tommy was a pervert, and Grandma Clara died before she could be a great-great grandmother.

At first, Rosso tried to comfort the women, but by the time he had dipped into his third-tier Smarthearts, he had learned that his rapid-fire serial dating attracted women who were playing the same high-risk game. He experienced a string of encounters so disastrous that even nature had the good sense to intervene. During a typical 3 a.m. boo-hoo, this time in Rosso's home, a mouse scurried over his date's pantyhose which, mercifully for Rosso, was still on her body when she ran out the door screaming.

At 6 Hillside, Mrs. Morris called the police to report what she insisted was a child molestation. Minutes later, the New Canaan police arrived, prepared to rough up Rosso for what they considered to be the most heinous crime known to man. Instead, the officers ended up driving Rosso's date home. After they had left, Rosso called the exterminator to book the earliest available appointment.

One week later, Rosso opened his e-mail, hoping for a word from Elizabeth Taylor. Instead, the only messages were from an uncommonly persistent Phoebe, who confirmed dinner that evening, and from the Belle of Amherst, who attached the following bio.

**Smartheart Inc.**

**Name:** Lauren Ziegler

**Occupation:** Health Professional

**Schools:** Amherst College

**Address:** Compo Road, Westport, Connecticut.

**Age:** 30 **Height:** 5'6"

**Status:** Single

**Children:** None

**Description:** Brown hair, hazel eyes

**Religion:** None

**Hobbies (in order of importance):** Hiking, biking, reading, writing.

**Favorite Books:** Anything by Emerson or Thoreau.

**What are you looking for in a companion?** Hiker, biker, reader, writer.

Health Professional sounded like a dodge, but Rosso saved her bio because granola-munching nature types were often sane —a mental commodity he no longer took for granted.

Rosso picked up Phoebe in New Canaan. From her window, he could see her working on whatever it was she worked on. Whatever it was seemed very interactive and extremely virtual.

Phoebe invited him in and Rosso immediately tripped over the countless stuffed animals in her menagerie: cats, dogs, lions, tigers, bears. A jungle in which she, the most awesome predator of all, padded around in her Tweetie slippers and thong underwear.

"Put some clothes on," Rosso cried. "I'm a defenseless, divorced, red-blooded, Italian-American!"

He unfastened his eyes from her long limbs, perfect buttocks, and skin so smooth his fingers imagined their touch. He turned to her bookcase, reaching for any title. The *Tibetan Book of the Dead* would do. His eyes skimmed past the rest of the books. They had nothing to talk about.

When he looked at her computer equipment, however, he was intrigued. Her gear was light years ahead of even the most advanced stuff he had seen demonstrated at trade shows or at the country's leading media labs. She had a 3-D sound system coupled with stereoscopic sunglasses. All this allowed her to dive into different worlds when, up until now, most people skimmed past the animated landscapes of their computer screens as if viewing a glass-bottomed boat. Her acoustigraphic environment had haptic feedback devices that created the illusion of substance and force within the virtual world. She could feel textures, as well as the pull of gravity. At the very least, Rosso thought, Phoebe might teach him something about her forays into cyberspace.

Charles had recommended Café de la Plage for dinner. The fish restaurant's commanding view of the Long Island sound, coupled with its romantic interior, had, Charles said, served him well as a Smartheart bachelor. His favorite waiter, Jean-Paul, had left, but he assured Rosso that Louis-François, his replacement, was every bit as good.

When Louis-François came to take their drink order, Phoebe asked for hot water. When Louis-François returned to take their dinner order, Phoebe asked for rice, lemon, and more hot water.

"Followed by?" Rosso looked at her, concerned that her apparent shyness—which he found appealing—would only result in her undernourishment. "Order anything you want," Rosso declared expansively. "My treat."

"Rice, lemon, and hot water," she repeated quietly.

Considerate too, Rosso thought. Not the kind of woman who sets out to ruin a man. He leaned over and whispered, "You can order *anything* on this menu."

"That's what I want," she whispered back.

"That's it?"

"That's it."

"Sure?"
"Sure"
"Positive?"
"Un huh."

Rosso suddenly wondered if she had one of those eating disorders that were in vogue—the thought of which made him change his order to something light. "I'll have the scampi," he said.

"Anything to start?" Louis-François asked, in an unsuccessful attempt to suppress his congenital Gallic irritation.

"No. That's it. You can bring my entrée at the same time you bring her…her…" He didn't know what to call it.

"Rice?" Louis-François offered.

"*Riz*," he countered.

After Louis-Francois had spun around on his heel and headed for kitchen, Rosso asked Phoebe if she was watching her weight.

"No. I'm purifying my body."
"Really?"
"Yes."
"Fasting?"
"How did you know?"

She seemed excited, as if Rosso had apprehended something profound about her.

"I take you to a nice restaurant on a first date and you're going too *fast* on me!"

"It's for spiritual reasons."
"Well what if fasting is against my religion?"
"Are you religious?"
"Yes."
"About food?"
"Devout."
"What religion is that?"
"Italian."

Rosso waved the waiter back to their table and stared at Phoebe as she began reciting the preamble for what turned out to be her more extensive discourse on belief. While she droned on, Rosso decided that Phoebe reminded him of Ursula Andress as Honeypot in the old James Bond movie. Louis-François handed Phoebe the menu *pour la deuxieme fois*, he muttered, and she scanned the offerings—*saumon en croute*, grilled sea bass, calimari, snapper—which, by now, Rosso had memorized. Then she looked up at Rosso, smiling sweetly.

She turned to Louis-François, momentarily disarming him as well, and said, "I'll have a hard-boiled egg, *oeuf dur*," she said, "but please have the chef remove the yolk." When there was no response from Louis-François, she continued, "I'm sorry. But I don't know how to say yolk in French."

After Louis-François had scurried back into the kitchen, what tumbled forth from Phoebe was a jumbled melange of Far Eastern beliefs and New Age idiosyncrasy. It went something like this.

In her first incarnation, she had been a mineral, then a plant, then an animal.

"Which mineral?"

"Zinc."

"What kind of plant?"

"Fern."

"What kind of animal?"

"Panther."

"So you've eaten meat."

"In past lives, yes. I've also been a man."

"Really?"

"I don't like your tone."

Rosso said he was sorry, but he was thinking, Take Me To Your Leader.

"I'm in a different life right now," she continued, looking disappointed. "I'm ruled by passion. It won't always be that way," she brightened. "My higher birth will allow me to develop my intellect."

At this point, Rosso considered asking Phoebe if, as a male, she had ever taken another soul, however irresistibly encased as a female, to dinner, only to have her order rice, lemon, hot water, and the albumen of an egg. But by then he thought it best to be silent. After all, he was now focused on one thing and one thing only. It was the baser, less enlightened form of Phoebe, comprised of X chromosomes, that he sought to please.

One hour later, when Rosso pulled into Phoebe's driveway, he was surprised when she asked him to come up.

"I'd love some coffee," he said politely. Despite his attraction, he had no intention of forcing his rabid heterosexuality on her.

Phoebe led Rosso into her apartment and immediately disconnected the QuickCam on top of her computer. "I don't have coffee," she said and turned suddenly to kiss him.

# 10

It was as if Phoebe's closet had a back door and that, when she opened it, it led somewhere and the where was of her choosing. An infinite number of possibilities for travel and experience presented themselves and, though some were frightening, she could say to herself, "I know the way home." She did not believe that aliens send earthlings home with implants, but sometimes her journeys were so real, they became part of her collective experience and profoundly influenced her daily life.

Phoebe insisted that Christ's second coming would occur in virtual reality.

Rosso said virtual reality was not the same as real life.

Phoebe said, "It's better."

Rosso said bullshit.

Rosso was beginning to miss Doris.

Doris was anything but virtual.

With Doris, Rosso *knew* what he was dealing with. Books were books. Glue was glue. The two stuck or didn't stick. Doris was happy. Doris was sad. Doris laughed when she was happy. Doris was a crybaby when she was sad. Doris was real.

Phoebe had seduced him. She had transported him to a

different world. "Virtual Reality's version of *The Lion, the Witch and the Wardrobe* and *Alice in Wonderland*," she explained. Each icon was like the window on an Advent calendar—only the windows were more like doors and there was no limit to the number of doors you could open and no end to the landscapes you could both choose from and inhabit.

Phoebe wanted to test a new program she had developed with her mentor, Dr. Lawrence Franz. A few seconds after it booted up, they were thrown into a sensory kaleidoscope which Phoebe found both spiritual and erotic. Geometric patterns blazed with the color of precious stones—rubies, emeralds, sapphires, topaz, and amethyst. They slid along iridescent spirals and landed inside corridors of light. Prism after prism conveyed them to the heart of a binary universe. The ecstasy had been experienced at *reckless* speeds, and when it stopped, the impact was sudden and terrible. Rosso had crashed. He was exhausted and shaking.

It was in this compromised state that Rosso felt Phoebe removing his gear. Her fingers wandered the length of his body, pressuring his muscles until the shaking stopped.

"Take off your shirt," she said.

And before he could even imagine doing so, Phoebe had unbuttoned, unzipped, and literally debriefed every secure point of entry on his Brooks Brothers clothing. Her tongue began darting feverishly down his body, probing, then mouthing everything in its path.

As Rosso disappeared inside her, their kiss sealed on a spasm. The next day, Rosso felt empty.

Though his body had a distinct memory of making love to Phoebe, the sensory foreplay which preceded it left him spent. It was impossible to retrieve or untangle a single skein of the more fragile emotions, which, for him, usually accompanied the most intimate of acts.

All this and more the confused Rosso tried to convey to Charles and Rita over brunch that Sunday.

"There are three types of men," Charles began and, instinctively, Rosso hailed the waiter. He ordered a Bloody Mary, though it would probably take at least two to steel himself against what he suspected was one of Charles's self-serving pontifications.

"The first has never experienced good sex and becomes enslaved by the first woman to perform a fellatial act."

"Good Lord, Charles!" Rita interrupted.

Charles smiled, stopping for a moment to order a Pimm's.

"My wife could use a Bloody Mary," he said to the waiter, who appeared reluctant to miss the rest of Charles's discourse.

"The second is starved for the companionship of a cultured woman and will ruin himself for a conversation about Nietszche."

Rosso looked at Rita and threw up his hands, as if to say, how could you *marry* this guy?

"The third simply plods on. He represents the innocent, unconscious mass of unfulfilled and anxiety-ridden hunter-gathers."

Rita laughed. "Which one are you?"

"And what's your fucking point?" Rosso asked.

"The point is that I consider all three types pathetic and that, until now, I thought you, like me, had escaped classification."

"You're such an elitist," Rosso said. "But thanks for kicking me out of your club. One's a crowd."

"What does all this have to do with Phoebe?" Rita asked. Charles's blank stare transformed itself into an irritated squint as he leaned towards Rosso and whispered, "Don't gild the lily."

"What's that supposed to mean?" Rosso asked.

"Phoebe's a *kook!*" Charles turned to Rita in despair, as if to say, help me on this one.

After a long pause, Rita, who was determined to tread gingerly on Rosso's feelings, said, "I'm suspicious of people who need props."

"Oh, for Chrissakes, *just turn the damn thing off!*" Charles cried.

"Turn *what* off?" Rosso asked.

"The computer. All that fancy equipment must have an on-off button."

"I can't believe you said that!" Rosso cried.

Rita couldn't either. On various occasions, both she and Rosso would have loved to turn off Charles's beeper.

Rita had fantasies about smashing its electronic vocal cords, about casting it into the pond behind their house, or burying it in the cemetery behind the local Rotary Club. Or just plain *turning it off.*

"Is that your amorous advice?" Rosso asked.

"Well, it *is* an option," Charles continued. "You can turn off your answering machine. You can turn off your television. You can turn the ringer off on your telephone." As if to reinforce his point, Charles started reciting his favorite anti-progress poem, one by Ted Hughes, which began with a "plastic Buddha jars out a Karate screech" and ended more ominously with "a flame from the last day will come lashing out of the telephone." So, intoning Hughes, Charles admonished, "*Do not pick up the telephone.*" When his cellular phone actually rang, Charles cried with a final flourish, "*A dead body will fall out of the telephone!*"

Had Rosso not been expecting the exterminator, he would have popped Charles one. Pompous ass. Quotes Ted Hughes and picks up his damn cellular phone because it's *his* phone, *his* LIFE and DEATH trauma. It was hard enough being divorced. And dating in an era when the world's entire single population seemed to have lost its senses was tough. But to be harangued by his smug, fat-headed friend was unendurable. Especially since part of Rosso, his unrepentant, less gentlemanly civilian side, wanted to shout "best sex I ever had," if only to provoke Charles.

Rosso knew that Phoebe was no Rita, but the larger point was that Charles didn't get it. *It's a jungle out here!* Rosso felt like shouting.

The larger picture was no better.

On the eve of this twenty-first century, which Rosso entered dispiritedly as a single man, there was still no peace in either the Middle East, Northern Ireland, Kosovo, East Timor, or Rwanda. Closer to home, the United States House of Representatives had impeached its forty-second president after he lied under oath about playing hide-the-cigar with a twenty-one-year-old intern in the Oval Office.

In this context, Rosso, a devout heterosexual, was an innocent. His Hebraic friends considered him a mensch; the Gentiles thought him a stand-up guy. To those who knew him best, he was a good man, a great catch, and, above all, the marrying kind.

Yet meeting an interesting women was proving far more difficult than Rosso had imagined.

How could he tell Charles that Jacqueline, the classy museum curator from Princeton, had refused to date him, *not* because he was white, but because he was *divorced*? Would Charles understand that the only singles over thirty-five who were remotely *compos mentis* had already been married? Could he believe that every Smartheart Rosso's age was taking Prozac, Lithium, or some other mood-altering cocktail? Finally, did he accept that, however absurd, Rosso honestly believed that his best candidate thus far was a woman from Boston he had never met?

Rosso *knew* how to meet women. The task was to find a woman like Rita, the very reason he had joined Smartheart. The only question Rosso needed an answer to was this: Where do the Ritas of the world gather?

Because he considered Rita the wisest former single person he knew, he asked her point blank, over dessert, in front of Charles.

"Try the Metropolitan," she suggested.

Charles guffawed into his napkin.

"Ignore him," Rita said, smacking her husband on the back of his head. "He's a boor."

"Which section?"

"Medieval," Rita offered.

Rosso pictured the museum's dimly lit cases with relics from the twelfth century. By medieval, he knew that Rita did not mean lances, chain mail, the stiffs in armor. She was probably referring to the ivories.

"The triptychs are *simply marvelous!*" Charles exclaimed, sounding like Julia Child pulling a perfect soufflé out of the oven.

"You are *such* an asshole," Rosso said.

Still, he had to admit, no fucking way he was going to hang out with the triptychs.

Back home, waiting for the exterminator, Rosso called up the international listings. The singles scene abroad could not possibly be as complex.

**Smartheart International, Inc.**
International Relief Worker (36) seeks commoner to
rescue her from Ivory Tower (London).

Since Rosso had a soft spot for people who do God's work, he called up her bio.

**Smartheart Inc.**

**Name:** Diana Spencer

**Schools:** Kindergarten Teacher

**Address:** South Kensington, London

**Occupation:** International Relief Worker

**Age:** 36 **Height:** 5'10"

**Description:** Blonde hair; blue eyes.

**Status:** Divorced

**Children:** Two

**Religion:** Protestant

**Hobbies (in order of importance):** Time with my boys, charity work, music, and fashion.

**Favorite Books:** Works of Astrology. Books by Contemporary Spiritual Thinkers.

**What are you looking for in a companion?** Monogamy, kindness, humor, and style.

Oh Christ. Poor Princess.

At the same time, he was annoyed with Smartheart International for failing to update its files.

Rosso remembered the summer of Diana's death. Technically, he and Doris had been separated, but they had had a few relapses. On the night of the first relapse, they had made love, after which Doris had turned on the eleven o'clock news to learn of Diana's crash in Paris. By morning, the princess was dead.

On the night of Doris's second relapse, she had reached over to set the alarm.

"What are you doing?" Rosso had asked.

"Diana's funeral is in the morning."

Charles had predicted that, with the burial of Diana, there would be no more relapses. With an air violin, he had played "A Candle in the Wind" in mock *lachrymosa*. Now, just thinking about Charles's response pissed Rosso off.

As he cleared his screen, Rosso vowed never again to share the details of his single life with anyone, especially Charles and Rita.

11

"Which one did you see?" the exterminator asked. He introduced himself as Sonny and held up *The Last Supper*'s MOST WANTED poster. Picture after picture, each one more unsavory than the other, the rogue's gallery of rodents was breaking Rosso's spirit.

"I think it was that one," Rosso said, pointing to a mouse. He looked at Sonny as if to plead, Lord, let it be a mouse.

Suddenly, Rascal's tail started wagging faster than the highest setting on Rosso's windshield wipers. A few seconds later, her brown tail batted like a flag marking another location. She scratched the garbage can and tried to swat it aside. A rat the size of a small raccoon ran for its life.

"Augh!" Rosso cried, then instantly reprimanded himself. Most unmanly for a Navy man.

Rosso followed Sonny around like an eager but conflicted pupil. He cheered him on, begging him to keep the rats out of the basement *by any means necessary*. Since ratting was a lonely profession, Sonny was happy to have Rosso in tow. He began by showing him the hole near the kitchen. He shook his head gravely. He spotted two more holes near the cellar door. Under the trash, he found another. When Rosso let him into the garage, Sonny looked in one corner and whispered "Gosh," then examined the opposite corner and muttered "Oh gosh." When it got to "Golly" followed by "Goll-eee!," an exasperated Rosso asked, "What *is* it!?"

Sonny pointed to the lawnseed bag in the corner. "They're having a feast in there," he said.

Rosso locked the garage behind them.

"Any dog poop in the yard?" Sonny asked.

"No."

"Good. It's caviar for rats."

When Sonny asked to check the basement, Rosso declined to follow. Instead, he started to picture a system of underground tunnels more elaborate than Harriet Tubman's. How much, Rosso wondered, would it take to flee this and other homeowner's nightmares—rodents, gutters, boilers, and yards? Ten minutes into Rosso's fantasy of moving back to New York City, he saw Mrs. Becker approach. In a perverse moment of triumph, Rosso told himself that the sight of an exterminator's truck should instantly lower the value of his house or, at the very least, threaten Mrs. Becker's commission. Instead, she waved Rosso over and said, "Go to Home Depot and get yourself some steel garbage cans."

After she left, Sonny re-emerged from the basement with a grin on his face. "No penetration," he said.

Rosso was relieved.

"Repulsive, aren't they?" Rosso said.

"Yes, sir. But smart as the dickens. And where there's one, there's a family."

"What happens next?"

"I'll need a beer," Sonny said. He pulled out a trap and two plastic bags of poison covered with warnings in bold.

"What's that?"

"A Zinc-based rodenticide." Sonny reached into his pest

control box, pulled out a jar of peanut butter, and smeared it inside the trap. "They love this stuff, " he said. He secured the poison next to the peanut butter and closed the box with a plastic key.

"I don't want to alarm you," he said quietly, patting the box, "but a simple mistake and you're dead within the hour."

With that, Sonny pulled out his company's pest control contract and asked if he had any more questions.

"What about Rascal?"

Rosso had agreed to sit while Doris and the Red Sock were at some resort discussing their breakup. Rascal appeared to understand the gravity of Rosso's thoughts. As if to say, "You wouldn't want to lose me now," she hurled her nose against Sonny's mouth and kissed him.

"I've had thirteen years' experience," he said, scratching Rascal behind the ears. "We've never lost a dog."

"Have you lost any rats?"

"Are you kidding?" Sonny said gaily. For the first time, Sonny smiled. Even more surprising was his raucous laugh, which reminded Rosso of Walter Huston in *The Treasure of Sierra Madre*. "We always get 'em!"

Just then Rosso noticed Sonny's left arm dangling straight down from his shoulder. It was short and unfinished, with no elbow, and looked like a flipper—the result, Rosso presumed, of his mother taking Thalidomide.

"Handicaps are a state of mind," Sonny said, noticing Rosso's quick glance. Then he asked again for the beer.

Rosso went into the kitchen, opened a Sam Adams, and offered it to Sonny.

"Why do you need beer?" he asked. Fair question since, last year, Rosso's handyman had drunk a case and painted his windows shut.

"If I put the poison in the hole, invert the bottle, push the beer bottle in with my heel, then crush the glass with a hammer, the rat will eat the poison and lacerate itself to death on the way up."

Rosso spit up the beer and the bubbles came flying out his nose. "Sorry," he said, wiping his face.

"Rats are an emotional matter," Sonny said. He was the only person Rosso had met who could get away with cliché after cliché, by virtue of the unimpeachable sincerity that underlay his every utterance and action.

Before Sonny left, he scribbled his home number on the tear-off portion of the contract and gave Rosso his card.

"What's this?" Rosso asked, pointing to the other side of his card.

"My night job."

"Security?"

"Yes, sir. I love ratting, but it doesn't pay the bills. It's the human pests that put my kids through school."

"What kind?"

"Stalkers, psychos, garden-variety perverts, and private detective stuff—divorce, surveillance, and missing persons. I'm not at liberty to talk about specific cases."

After Sonny left, Rosso took Rascal for a run. She was too little to jog alongside, so, as an experiment, Rosso nestled her in the bucket of a three-wheel, double-jogging stroller he had just bought for Charles and Rita. Babies bellowed "PUPPY!" as they sped by. Parents smiled, then conferred with each other: Who do we know? He's *obviously* ready.

As Rosso approached his garage, he was thinking that, of all the women he had met in the last few months, Rascal, whom Rosso had only known a few weeks, was the most affectionate, the most constant, and the most fun. The only candidate who remotely matched Rascal in spirit and insight was Elizabeth Taylor, who, to Rosso's despair, he had neither been able to reach nor forget. Still, Rosso held to his stubborn hope, though with regard to looks, once again Liz was a complete unknown. "What if she's a woofer?" Charles had asked. Rascal, with her copper coat and lambent eyes, clearly was not.

As Rosso approached his mailbox, he caught a movement in Mrs. Selby's window. He had noticed her watching him from behind the curtain for months, especially on days a beat-up subcompact stood parked in her gravel driveway. When Eugenia Fishman Selby rushed out the door, pulling a young woman by the hand, the reason for her vigil became as clear as the spectacular, dappled, and unseasonably warm autumn day that helped produce the encounter.

"This is my daughter, Sandra. She lives in New York City."

"Hello Sandra," Rosso said.

"Hello," she replied, reaching over to pet Rascal. "Cute puppy."

"She's not married." Mrs. Selby winked.

"I'm divorced," Rosso said, in an effort to repel the mother and side with Sandra, who struck Rosso as a really good sport. "I'm sure your mother has warned you about divorced men."

"I did, but I'm desperate," Mrs. Selby said. Her rare moment of candor produced an involuntary tickle. She began to laugh the laugh of a woman who never laughed, the brittle, high-strung, demented laugh of a neurotic mother releasing years of pent-up fears about herself and her daughter. Finally, even Sandra, who appeared vastly more mature than her mother, smiled in spite of herself.

Rosso found himself smiling too. This was not the first time he had been approached by a mother. The truth was that mothers loved Rosso—big mothers, little mothers, Jewish mothers, WASP mothers, divorced mothers, married mothers, single mothers, widowed mothers, white mothers and black mothers. Rosso was the kind of guy they saw married to their daughters. While Rosso was grateful for their constituency, he wondered if their dateworthy offspring needed a mother to procure for them. Rosso assumed that an interesting, desirable woman would probably be fighting men off.

After Rosso had excused himself, he headed for his mailbox. The black metal hutch with its red flag was always a welcome sight—especially when it was bursting with mail. He did some of his best thinking on the way to and from the mailbox.

He began to wonder. How do you let a nutcase like Phoebe down gently?

He opened his mailbox.

Maybe Phoebe was a sexual cyborg, a human enhanced by technology.

He reached for his mail.

The everyday netter was no better. Rosso wondered if people would still make spectacles of themselves if anonymity weren't, in the Net's infancy, so prevalent.

He flipped through his mail.

An envelope from his sister commanded his attention. She had scrawled, in huge letters, *URGENT*, with the italic felt tip she usually reserved for Christmas cards. Inside was a newspaper clipping about Phoebe's mentor. Rosso was touched by his sister's thoughtfulness, but he soon grew alarmed. Up top, she had written in red, *"Be careful. Sounds like a psycho!"*

**Gurus In Cyberspace**
© Associated Investigations

By day, students of Dr. Lawrence Franz work as computer consultants and graphic artists. But their full time spiritual life is devoted to preaching Dr. Franz's path to enlightenment through computer science. Hundreds of brilliant and mostly young professionals, including engineers, musicians, and videographers, are charged thousands of dollars each to belong to what experts are calling a cult. "He gets smart people to do stupid things," says Sri Limnoy, a guru from Astoria, Queens who was once Dr. Franz's teacher.

Like most cults, Franz's path to enlightenment cuts people off from their past and forbids them to give their home numbers to friends or family outside the group. Members are often recruited through free meditation seminars and trained in computer programming. Franz uses computers to focus the mind, while isolating the body.

"He's not interested in exploring the fluid boundary between humans and technology," says Dr. Susan Pinker, a professor of science at M.I.T. "He doesn't allow individuals to explore how their identities might be changed or enhanced. It's a perversion of what we try to do here. Franz is simply out to control people's minds."

Franz's group has never been convicted of any crime, but five of his students have committed suicide, while seventeen others have disappeared.

Franz, who claims to be fully enlightened and who goes by the name Vishnu, owns nine sports cars and is reported to sleep with several of his female students at a time.

## 12

The twelfth of November marked Rosso's thirty-ninth birthday. His mother had called, broadsiding him with the announcement that she and Gus were engaged. Charles and Rita confirmed dinner at Café de la Plage. He accepted their offer, but wondered if he had enough social energy. To him, the day meant that he had outlived his father. Depressing to arrive at thirty-nine, only to realize just how young his father had been.

For the better part of a week, Phoebe had been calling and e-mailing Rosso, thanking him for the date, and wondering when they might get together. Until now, Rosso had been ducking her, hoping she would go away. But he sensed that Phoebe had not given up, that she actually admired his lack of cult potential. And he wanted to be clear.

Rosso told himself that, mercifully, his encounter with Phoebe had not constituted a relationship. He didn't know how to classify it. An online flirtation, yes. A collision, definitely. A one-night stand, absolutely. But certainly not a relationship.

He resolved that it was curtains for Phoebe. No letting her down softly. No let's be friends. No recreational sex. And no waiting for the *60 Minutes* exposé on Franz. Everybody makes mistakes, Rosso told himself. However sudden, it was time to nip this nutter in the bud.

Rosso called Phoebe from his car phone and invited her to lunch. In the meantime, he did a quick search, after which, he felt like an idiot.

Phoebe had not gone to Brown. College records, transcripts, and yearbook photos did not exist. According to Dave Minton, the co-founder of Smartheart, whom Rosso advised of the fraud, Phoebe had submitted a copy of the alumni magazine's address label as proof of matriculation. Dave apologized, adding that he had been overwhelmed by the success of Smartheart. The dating network he had founded with Louise was expanding too quickly—especially with regard to Smartheart's new website. Small Ivies and Seven Sister schools were legitimate, but hotel management grads from Cornell and other Ivy wannabees were slipping through the net. He reassured Rosso that they were addressing the problem and confessed that he longed for the early days, when he and Louise would screen candidates, issue membership numbers, send out monthly lists, and process requests for the modest fee of six dollars for a full-length bio.

When Rosso voiced his misgivings about Smartheart International, Dave admitted it had spun out of control ever since he had sold his rights to a cousin of the Windsors. To his regret, the international chapter had become a dating service for celebrities, actors, and washed-up royals. When no diploma was available, Smartheart International was accepting a crest.

Rosso figured that Phoebe had subscribed to the magazine and had it sent to her home. The only point of confusion in Phoebe's otherwise straightforward deceit was that the address on the alumni magazine's label did not match the apartment Rosso had visited. Instead, it led to a beach house owned by Franz. All this and more Rosso intended to bring up over water, rice, and, no doubt, the god-awful, ever-repugnant, and obliging hard-boiled egg, *sans* yolk.

Rosso made his way to Westport and pulled into the only space in front of Pal Joey. What the diner lacked in decor, it made up for in cuisine—the same mom and pop Greek couple had been cooking superb dishes for twenty-five years. Rosso looked up from the menu to see his neighbor, Mr. Williams, order a coffee and muffin before heading out to play golf.

"Sorry about the golf incident," Mr. Williams said.

"I'm the one who owes you an apology," Rosso insisted. "Marital discord," he explained, shaking Mr. Williams's hand. There were too many loose ends in modern life, Rosso thought, though happily this time. A full two months later, they sometimes tied themselves up simply, with a chance encounter in a local coffee shop.

Mr. Williams heard the chimes on the door and turned to see a young woman lumber in like a colt who had just found her legs. Another complication in a young man's life, Mr. Williams deduced. He smiled and said, "Call me when you want to play golf."

Phoebe fell sideways into a chair and Rosso wasted no time. "You didn't go to Brown, Phoebe. And you've never set foot in Providence."

Phoebe dismissed his comment. It was of no consequence to her. "We need to spend more time together," she said.

Then more phrases started coming. Any man can recite them with greater accuracy than he can his own name, rank, and serial number. *You don't listen to a word I say. You don't take my feelings seriously.* Then came the inevitable zinger, which, sadly for Phoebe, was not only moot but reflected her tenuous grasp on reality. *I want to know where this relationship is headed.*

Over the last few months, Rosso had noticed that women often wanted their entire destiny with a man sewn up after a few dates. Since Rosso had known Doris for years before they married, this impossible acceleration of intimacy made Rosso feel incidental to the larger machinery of a woman's will.

I could be anybody, Rosso thought.

After Joey delivered their food, Rosso leaned over his *moussaka* and asked, "Is Franz using you to infiltrate Smartheart for new recruits?"

"I don't know what you're talking about."

"Phoebe," he said, catching her volleying glance. "Five of his followers have committed suicide and seventeen are missing."

"That's a bunch of crap."

"How so?"

"They were spiritually lost."

"Jesus, Phoebe! What does it take —Kool-Aid?"

But Phoebe had never heard about Jim Jones and the mass suicide in Guyana.

"I have no interest in dating you, Phoebe," Rosso said plainly. "I never will."

Phoebe's eyes started to water, but she took the hit.

"Listen," Phoebe urged. Her voice was humorless. "You've *got* to tell me who else you've been dating."

"Are they in danger?"

"No."

"Are you?"

Phoebe's eyes wandered from one item on the table to the next. In one violent sweep, she cleared the table with her arm. Plates, glasses, creamers, and shakers came to a shattering finish. While Rosso bent down to clean up the mess, Phoebe reached for her purse and ran out.

That night, before dinner, an unexpected birthday present arrived in the form of a conversation with Elizabeth Taylor online.

JR: Why Elizabeth Taylor?
Liz: Cause people always say I look like the young Liz.

JR: I admire her acting.
Liz: Me too. What range!
JR: From Cleopatra to *Who's Afraid of Virginia Woolf*.
Liz: To Wilma Flintstone.
JR: From Richard Burton—
Liz: To Larry Fortensky!
JR: A complex woman. That's why I watch old movies.
Liz: I don't follow.
JR: I'm trying to find out what women want.
Liz: Especially complex women?
JR: Yes.
Liz: By watching old movies?
JR: They were more complex then.
Liz: The women or the movies?
JR: The movies. The women were always complex.
Liz: So what have you learned?
JR: Women are looking for that James Dean, Richard Burton, Montgomery Cliff poetic heat—
Liz: Not bad.
JR: Combined with that help-me, help-me, save-me-from-myself and forgive-me-when-I-hurt-you self-destructive charm.
Liz: Much less appealing.
JR: Yes, but the two often go together.
Liz: Women love a broken wing?
JR: Some kind of maternal thing?
Liz: Perhaps.
JR: Yeah, but why do some men and women prefer people with broken wings?
Liz: Because they'll never fly away.
JR: So people who tend to birds with broken wings are never alone.
Liz: They can't be alone. That's the point. Screwed up people are never alone.

JR: So screwed up people are better off?

Liz: Not necessarily.

JR: Do you think that some people are together because they're terrified of being alone?

Liz: Of course.

JR: You're so matter of fact about it.

Liz: It's so obvious.

JR: In your opinion, what kind of man does Hollywood offer as an alternative?

Liz: Spencer Tracy, Jimmy Stewart, and Tom Hanks. Hollywood offers women men they can count on. I've got to go.

JR: WAIT! Can we meet?

"Happy Birthday, " Charles smiled. He sat alone. Midway though his martini, he signaled the waiter. "One white wine for my wife. " He turned to Rosso. "What does the birthday boy want?"

Rosso sank into his chair and rubbed his eyes. "A deprogrammer." He looked up and smiled wearily at their waiter. "Louis-Francois almost ruined my first date with Phoebe."

"What commendable insight!" Charles quipped. He waved at Rita, who was making her way to the table.

"I'll have Sam Adams," Rosso said.

"Sorry I'm late," Rita smiled. "Happy Birthday!" she said, leaning over to kiss Rosso.

Louis-Francois reached for her coat, snapping his fingers to summon the coat check girl.

"We have cause to celebrate," Charles said, holding up his glass. "My beeper's off and Jim has dumped Fifi."

"Phoebe," Rita corrected. She clapped a hand over her mouth to suppress a laugh.

"Christ, Charles. Do you ever remember your *patients'* names?"

"I remember their operations!" Charles cried buoyantly.

Rita examined Rosso's face. "She wasn't for you," she said.

"To be honest with you, I couldn't get past the eggs," Charles said suddenly, roaring with laughter.

For Rita, as for Rosso, Charles's wild moments of spirit and abandon redeemed his otherwise restrained temperament. Rita was holding her table napkin like a veiled dancer. Her eyes danced above its rim and, though she tried to muffle it, her rich laugh coaxed Rosso out of his momentary irritation. After a few more jags of laughter, Charles asked, "What ever happened to Liz Taylor?"

"Elizabeth Taylor!?" Rita cried.

"Have you learned her real name?"

Don't leave yourself open, Rosso reminded himself. He tried turning the tables around. "Don't you guys have a life?"

"For some reason, Rita finds yours far more interesting." Charles smiled. He waved a breadstick in front of Rita's eyes, as if testing her unresponsive pupils. "You don't like Elizabeth Taylor?"

"I do," she said, forcing a smile. "But I'm concerned. It sounds like a fantasy."

"Oh, for Chrissakes, honey, don't say that! He'll go back to Doris."

"Doris!?"

"You heard me." Charles pretended to bind the menu, so painstakingly that even Rosso smiled.

"I have nothing to disclose," Rosso said.

"That's true," Charles said, in a good-natured effort to provoke Rosso. "He hasn't met 'Liz' yet."

"Then you can't possibly know," Rita said.

"Yes I can." His tone was unusually curt.

"How?" Rita persisted.

"Ask Charles. He'd decided after the first date."

"Ah, but you're no Charles Dine," Charles said, shaking his finger at Rosso.

"And there was a first date," Rita added.

"Because it's my birthday. That's how I know," Rosso said, aborting the line of inquiry. "End of story!"

Rita watched Louis-Francois approach the table in a swift, swirling motion, as if unencumbered by feet.

"Do you know what you want?" Rita asked Rosso.

"Yes, I believe I do," Rosso said, almost defiantly.

By then, Louis-Francois was standing in front of Rosso.

"For *dinner*," Rita said.

# 13

The dense foliage of the lower Hudson Valley gave Rita the feeling she was driving through a leafy tunnel, sometimes lofty as a cathedral, other times dark and oppressive. The Hudson rolled wide and as slow as the Mississippi in some parts and, farther south, Sing Sing, the high security prison, loomed like a fortress over the river's churlish waters.

Rita pulled into the driveway of her parents' house, a white colonial with red shutters. As she unbuckled her children's carseats, she heard the joyous greetings of her parents who, sensing their daughter's exhaustion, had offered to take Rita's children for the day.

After feeding her children lunch, Rita wandered upstairs and sat on the twin bed she had slept in for the better part of her childhood. She had always dreaded staying too long in the room, but this time she got up and moved to the chair in front of her small Formica desk. She pulled the top drawer open and confronted its contents as if they could make sense of her life. A chip of mica from summer camp twenty-five years before. Laces for a pair of skates that in a few years would fit her son.

Ticonderoga pencils so old their erasers smeared words before breaking off into hard rubber pellets. A photograph of her mother beaming as she held Rita in the maternity ward. A picture of her father when he was sixteen, arms flexed like Tarzan, grinning before he dove into the Hudson.

She moved from the desk to the seat in front of the vanity her mother had given her on her sixteenth birthday. There, in the mirror, she caught an expression that frightened her—one she recognized from the disappointed, bitter community of unloved people she had both dreaded and vowed never to become.

The faces of the men and women who took their partners back following an infidelity bore the mark of resignation, sorrow, and blighted self-esteem. The practical aspects of the return, often unassailable, involved finances, children, and sometimes even social mores. But the murder of a spirit always seemed to Rita too steep a price to pay for domestic equilibrium. She had watched her friends' marriages split up and sew themselves back together with apparent seamlessness, when really a basting stitch was all that kept them from the more honest rip. Sometimes the extracurricular affair bore out to be nothing more than a fantasy—the unconsummated freedom of a man or a woman who had married too early. This sort of affair was easily identified by weekend getaways without children, passionate notes delivered through office e-mail, a disproportionate attention to lingerie, and a sudden blindness to the loved one's abuse of alcohol, tobacco, food, or any other excess.

The more troubling affairs had to do with love. It was this kind of affair Rita suspected her husband had possessed. The fact that the woman had been his patient was of no consequence to her; nor, just then, was she particularly curious about the circumstances under which they had met. Anne and Charles had been soulmates. That much she could sense, and what could be more intimate?

One hour later, Rita set off for New York City. Three miles into the drive, she found herself heading in the opposite direction; the car seemed to be driving itself. The closer she got to the familiar place, the more she had difficulty breathing. She did not know if the man she had once loved still lived in the log cabin at the top of the hill. It had been nine years since she had last seen Jack. She had heard about his marriage, he had written to her of his divorce, and she had read a small but favorable review of his primer for young playwrights.

As she approached on the winding road, a few miles from Bear Mountain, Rita spotted Jack pruning a tree that touched the telephone wires. He had grayed a bit, but his lithe and powerful build still cut a seductive profile. He looked towards the car and climbed down from the ladder when his visitor pulled up in front of the house. Only when she opened the door could he make out who had come. He stopped to catch his breath. "Good God, Rita, " he exclaimed softly. "You haven't changed a bit."

Rita wandered through Jack's garden, surveying the many plantings that had grown heartily in her absence. Her favorite azalea was still there. In the summer, it bloomed a hot-pink so intense that the neighboring hydrangea, white but rinsed with green, seemed necessary to soothe the eye.

Jack was overwhelmed by Rita's presence. So much so that he, who in his years on stage had always been rebellious, suddenly discovered the practical aspect of good manners. "Can I get you some coffee?" he asked, thinking that if Rita said no he would go mad.

Inside, he held the coffee spout over Rita's cup and poured. It was all so silent. All so familiar. Rita spilled the coffee, not much, but enough to stain the cheerful tablecloth by turning one of its wild roses brown.

"Ugh," Rita shuddered as she wiped her eyes brusquely. "What a mess!"

"What's wrong? " Jack asked. His manner was grave.

"I don't have the stomach for this," she said, popping up suddenly and stepping out the screen door. She walked briskly, heading for her favorite trail. She was thinking that she had made a selfish, confused, impulsive, and terrible mistake by visiting Jack.

She walked until dusk. Clouds of pink tractor treads illuminated the sky and winter flowers on either sides of the path punched color into an otherwise mulchy brown trail. From behind, she felt a stem slide down her neck. Then she reached for what turned out to be a petal and trampled it underfoot. Jack, who had caught up with her, picked up an acorn and started all over again. These coded ways of expressing affection seemed to Rita unendurable acts of provocation. Five minutes into the charade, Rita's fury got the best of her. She stopped cold. Jack stumbled against her. "Don't!" she said, pushing him away as he tried to enfold her in his arms.

The edge in her voice arrested his ardor. She ran on ahead, well out of reach, well out of earshot.

Minutes later, Jack caught up with her. "I'm sorry," he said.

Rita stared into Jack's eyes. "My children are the most important people in my world," she said.

"They're lucky."

"I mean it," she said.

"I know. I wasn't mocking you."

She wanted to talk to him about everything. Her work, her marriage, and Charles. She wanted to say that her husband had been in love with another woman for the duration of their marriage. She wanted to talk about her son, who showed no sign of speaking. She wanted to say that her unwitting flirtations online would destroy her friendship with Rosso, on whom she relied. Instead she said, "This was a mistake," did an about-face, and headed back towards the car.

"Rita!" Jack caught up with her. "Don't leave like this."

"I'm sorry," she said, repeating the words time and time again. "Do you want me to tell you how often I think of you?"

"No."

"Well, I need to tell you. I want you to know how much you are missed. Please come inside for a minute."

"I can't."

"I won't keep you."

Jack stopped himself from touching her as they made their way to the den.

Rita settled into the beat-up leather chair on which she had spent many an evening and, suddenly, the full weight of her past roared overhead like a wave and crushed her the minute she looked at Jack.

"I can't breathe!" she cried, jumping up again. She was conscious that her behavior was ridiculous and hysterical, but, somehow, truly honest.

"I really am sorry, Jack. I have to leave."

Jack followed her into the garden, where even the plants seemed too intimate a memory. She walked towards the car and turned to say goodbye.

"I'm sorry. My children need—"

"Oh for God's sake, Rita. Cut it out!"

"Cut what out?" she asked angrily.

"You haven't discovered maternity. Stop using your kids as an excuse!"

"I'm not."

"Yes, you are!"

"Excuse for *what*?" she demanded.

"For a mistake you made."

"Don't talk to me about mistakes, " she shouted. "Your life is full of them!"

"You're right! So *what?*" he laughed, throwing up his hands.

"Your life's one big mistake!" she screamed. "You can't even begin to understand what it feels like to love someone more than you love yourself!"

"Oh, get off your high horse."

She opened the car door and threw her purse onto the passenger seat. He grabbed her arm and slipped behind her, into the driver's seat.

"Just let me hold you," he said, pulling her onto his lap.

"I'm too mad!" she yelled, pushing her way out of the car. She shoved him with all her force. He hit his head on the rearview mirror and fell against her purse.

Rita stood outside waiting. Ten seconds later, she muttered, "Come on, Jack." After thirty seconds, she cried, "Get up!" When his head slid over the edge of the seat, she began to worry. "Are you okay?" she asked. His eyes were closed and his breathing was shallow. When Rita got no response, she started to shake him. He whipped his head around and smiled the gentle, mischievous smile that had seduced her more than ten years before.

"Damn you!" she shouted. She noticed a bump on his head, but otherwise he was fine.

He crawled into the driver's seat and put his arms around her. "I'm not going to let you go that easily."

"You've done it before!"

"You dumped a playwright for a surgeon," he said.

"I don't blame you, so don't blame me.

Rita whispered something he could not make out. He placed his ear alongside her mouth, as if to catch it. When she did not repeat herself, Jack sighed and held her closer.

"You've been very brave, Rita." He waited for her to look at him. Tears rolled down her cheeks and dripped onto the hand that held hers. "I know you have children. I know you have a husband, and I know what all this means. But you have this hold on me," he said. "So don't come here unless you're prepared to change your life."

## 14

Rosso reviewed his options.
Phoebe was out.
Elizabeth Taylor remained a fantasy.
Belle of Amherst was a dubious candidate.
But Rosso was completely burned out.

He was the worst kind of loser, he told himself—getting into catfights with good guys like Sam; agreeing to dates with airheads; harboring hope for unavailable women; and consenting to a post-divorce custody agreement for his ex-wife's dog.

For three weeks, Rosso continued to beat himself up. He thought about branding a big L on his forehead, and putting himself out to pasture. He was good marriage material but an abysmally lousy dater. During this time, he renounced women, sent his mother an engagement present, finished his Rockefeller biography, played thirty-six holes of golf with Mr. Williams, and to the delight of his boss, brought in six new clients.

Rosso had adjusted to the peaceful, temperate, and celibate life of a Connecticut bachelor when he received a call from Jeff Reed. Since Paradise Island, Jeff had been on the road promoting a kind of driver's license for cyberspace known as digital certificates. He called to say that he couldn't get Future Systems e-mail from his home computer. By the time Rosso arrived at his office, the receptionist was overwhelmed with calls. "Something's wrong," she said.

Rosso logged on and was greeted by headshots of women he had dated. What's more, the attacker had defaced his company's website.

Employees began calling from hotel rooms all over the country. They couldn't connect to the mail server at Future Systems to receive their e-mail.

Hersh popped out of his office, as jumpy as a chicken at a barbecue. "The whole system's gone kaflooey!" he screamed.

Rosso was punching out keyboard commands, staring at his computer screen and, his habit when every second counted, reverting to military crisis speak. "Requesting permission to sever the Ethernet cable, sir."

"Permission denied!" Hersh yelled. "You'll cut off our goddamn internet access!"

"Who cares!" Rosso shouted. "Someone's trying to shut us down!" Just as Rosso was about to disconnect, another figure invaded his screen—a devil ripping out a human tongue.

"Mayday! Mayday!" Rosso cried. He severed the cable and ran to Future System's administrative computer, where he tried to reboot from the console. Too late. The attacker had taken control of the company's system. Rosso banged the computer and shouted every obscenity known to man.

The safest thing would be to shut the system down, wipe clean every computer in the network, reinstall every program, and change all the passwords. The system would be shut down for days.

"Requesting permission to shut down the system, sir."

When Hersh said no, Rosso grabbed the nearest phone and called Mike August, a former Navy buddy who was investigating break-ins for the supremely understaffed FBI. Rosso described the problem, handed Hersh the phone, and signed off with August, saying, "Tell my boss what he doesn't want to hear."

While Hersh spoke with August, dozens of computer screens suddenly flashed with the image of Rascal, bloody and battered beyond recognition.

"NO!" Rosso moaned.

He closed down the system and ran out of the building.

From his cell phone, Rosso called Doris. Just as well she could not see him. He was in his car, on 95, wiping hot tears from his eyes with the back of his sleeve.

"Where's Rascal?" he asked.

"Right here, licking my feet."

A few seconds passed in silence.

"Thank God," Rosso said softly.

Still, he was deeply unnerved. Whoever had broken in had been watching him. That same person had access to his files.

"What happened?" Doris asked.

"Some nutcase hacked into our office system."

"What does that have to do with Rascal?"

"He sent a disturbing image."

Doris was quiet. She did not really want to know. Rosso did not want to worry her. Once, early in their marriage, Rosso had put her under surveillance when a headhunter had turned out to be, well, literally, a headhunter. Whatever the circumstances, Doris knew that Rosso would protect her.

"You'll give him trouble?" she asked brightly, playing Guinevere to his Lancelot.

Rosso smiled. "He will be rubble."

"You'll open-wide him?"

"I'll sub-divide him."

"You'll disconnect him?"

"I'll vivisect him."

Countless times during their marriage, when they had agreed that human refuse should be banished from the earth, they had cribbed these lyrics from *Camelot*.

Rosso missed the shared references of marriage.

At 12 Hillside, Rosso checked the backup tapes he kept in his home office. He was relieved to find them in place. The good news in his otherwise turbulent day was that the Future Systems attacker had been sloppy. Three hours after the attack, one of Rosso's companies reported a suspicious caller trying to break in. Rosso turned on a sniffer, which logged the attacker's every move. He was confident that the logs would provide enough detail to eventually trace the source. Rosso suspected Franz. But he lacked the digital equivalent of a smoking gun. To the untrained eye, the painstaking task of investigating the break-in appeared about as interesting as preparing tax returns. But Rosso looked forward to it. This was war, after all, and he was going to win.

Three days after the attack, when Future Systems computers were up and running, Hersh asked to see Rosso. The meeting was at 10 a.m. and, while Rosso was catching up on his correspondence at home, his mailbox icon blinked. He clicked on it, trusting no one. The sender identified herself as the French woman Rosso had offended.

> *I devoted my youth to men. I dedicate the best years of my life to animals.*

Despite his days of mounting agitation, something about that line compelled him. He signed on to Smartheart's International website to see if her bio was available.

**Smartheart Inc.**

**Name:** B.B.

**Occupation:** Animal Rights Activist

**Schools:** L'Ecole de la Vie

**Address:** St. Tropez, France

**Age:** (don't be rude) **Height:** 5'9"

**Status:** Multiply-divorced

**Children:** One

**Description:** Blonde hair; blue eyes.

**Religion:** Catholique

**Hobbies (in order of importance):** All animals; some men.

**Favorite Books:** *Memoirs d'une Jeune Fille Rangée*, Simone de Beauvoir; *All Creatures Great and Small*, James Herriot.

**What are you looking for in a companion?** Humor, love of animals, and joie de vivre.

Rosso sent an instant message, in the event B.B. was still online.

*Did you take that line from Brigitte Bardot?*

Within seconds, she replied.

*I am Brigitte Bardot.*

When Rosso had recovered from his amazement, he dashed off an inquiry to the empress of the animal kingdom, the *ancienne* lover of Beatty, Belmondo, Vadim, and Brando, the champion of all critters, the beauty of her day whose soul, to this day, was as rare, as precious, and as brilliant as a diamond.

He wondered what Bibi would say about the psycho sending him revolting images.

Minutes later, she replied, mostly in English. With help from his translation software, he made out the rest.

*People who torture animals are dangerous. The tongue being ripped out by a devil is a medieval symbol for the vice of slander. Have you spoken ill of anyone lately?*

## 15

Rosso was on his way to the office, worrying about his meeting with Hersh. Since losing his wife to breast cancer, his boss was as unpredictable as the putter he had given him. When he was gruff, his enormously bushy salt-and-pepper eyebrows took on a life of their own—rising and falling or batting and bashing the object of their regard. Other times, Hersh was friendly. *Too* friendly. At Sawgrass, they had once been stuck in the same bunker on the seventeenth hole. After three tries, when Hersh had finally pitched his ball out, he put his arm around Rosso's shoulder and said, "Life just isn't worth living without the love of a good woman." Rosso was so rattled, he took a two-stroke penalty and threw his ball on the green.

Hersh's ursine affability made clients feel that he would take care of them. In an industry sleek and technical to the point of coldness, Hersh was a refreshing throwback to the owner of a corner store. The difference was that Hersh had kept up with the times. He had amassed a huge fortune, though not at the expense of his employees. If anything, Hersh had developed a failsafe formula for luring the best people in the field. He paid them well, guaranteed a generous retirement plan, built a state-of-the-art health club, and treated every one of his employees like a member of his family.

Hersh was cleaning a rifle from his hunting collection when his secretary showed Rosso in. By this time, Rosso had prepared himself for the worst. His private life was veering out of control.

"If you want a future with this company, Jim, you're going to have to pick your battles."

"Yes, sir."

Hersh took aim in the viewfinder and pointed the gun's barrel at Rosso. "I don't care what you do in your private life as long as you're not putting Future Systems in jeopardy."

"I understand, sir."

Hersh cocked the gun. "Unfair match to boot. You're a former officer, Rosso?"

"Yes, sir."

"And you pick a fight with a yellow-bellied, sprout-munching mamma's boy who probably wears the flag on his boxers."

"I've always had an aversion to cult figures, sir."

Hersh put his finger on the trigger.

"I wonder if you might put down the gun, sir."

"What's that? " Hersh's head poked out from behind the viewfinder.

"I said, please put the gun down."

Hersh was jarred into consciousness. "Sorry, Rosso! My wife used to hate it too. Second nature to me. You're a military man."

"I was, sir—"

"Jeff says you played hockey."

"That's right—"

"Bobby Orr's a personal friend of mine. I'll take you to meet him some time."

"My idol, sir."

Hersh pointed to the photograph on the wall. "China Beach."

SINGLE, WHITE CAVEMAN

He stood at attention and saluted Rosso, who instinctively saluted back.

"At ease," Hersh commanded, though Rosso, in the military at least, had outranked him. Hersh put his rifle back on the rack and rummaged through a drawer containing discontinued computer accessories, some of which had been rejected after test market research.

"You called the FBI," Hersh said, pulling out a trackball that mimicked a glass eye. He studied Rosso for a moment as he rolled the eye between his palms. "Who do you know there?"

"An old Navy buddy, sir."

"You're the only employee of ours who's ever been linked to an investigation through a girlfriend!"

"Ex-girlfriend. I'm sorry, sir."

Hersh channeled his agitation to the eyeball. With every bounce, he grew more determined that it land on its iris. "Took the FBI *seventeen goddamn years* to find that Unabomber!"

"That was unfortunate, sir."

"*Unfortunate*! He was after people like *me*. I could have been blown up!" Hersh eyed Rosso suspiciously. "Do you own a dog?"

"Yes, sir. Correction. No, sir."

"Do you or don't you!?"

"My ex-wife does."

"Rosso, your personal life's a mess!"

"Yes, sir."

"Back to the mindbender, Franz," Hersh said, reaching into his drawer for another knick-knack. "Do you have proof of his break-in?"

"Evidence, yes. Proof, no."

Hersh pulled out a motherboard and trimmed the nail on his pinkie with its serrated edge. When he had finished, he pulled a picture frame from behind his chair and slammed it on the desk.

"Now, *those* are dogs!"

Rosso stood still, as if expecting the first round of bullets from his executioner. When he opened his eyes, a portrait of three labs—one yellow, one chocolate, the other black, sat nobly by a proud Hersh.

"I said, those are dogs, Rosso! What do you say!?"

"Yes, sir."

"I can't *hear* you!"

"I said, YES, sir, those are dogs! The most noble breed in all the canine kingdom, sir."

"No Bichon, Poodle, or Pomeranian pufftas!"

"No, sir!"

"What kind of dog is Rascal?"

"A lab, sir."

"Color?"

"Chocolate."

"And what does dog spell backwards!?"

Rosso hesitated. Hersh eyed Rosso.

"God, sir."

"You're *goddamn right* it does!"

When Hersh appeared satisfied that Rosso was like-thinking, he gently returned his dogs to the shelf behind his desk.

"Sir, if I may," Rosso said, completely baffled by the conversation which had just taken place, "I'd like to know straightaway if you intend to fire me."

"Fire you?"

"Yes, sir."

"Whatever gave you that idea!? Goddamn bonkers, that's what you are!" Hersh roared, laughing with force enough to produce tears. "Fire you!?" He grabbed his gun-cleaning rag and wiped his eyes. "I'm promoting you to managing director!"

"Managing Director!?"

"That's right. You're doing a helluva job!"

"I'll do *better* work, sir."

"You've done just fine. Oh, I know, you keep odd hours and

you like the ladies, but I'd rather have you getting stuff done than have some sycophantic cocksucker work a hundred-hour week with less to show for it."

"Thank you, sir."

"Why do you keep calling me sir!"

"Vestige from the military when called in for questioning, sir."

"Managing directors don't call me sir, they call me Bob."

A bewildered Rosso left Hersh's office. Good-hearted as his boss was, Rosso wondered if he didn't have a few bats in the belfry.

# 16

When Lauren "Belle of Amherst" Ziegler called in lieu, she said, of answering the e-mail Rosso had sent weeks before, he begged off meeting her. In part, Rosso was cultivating the instincts of a seasoned dater. Lauren, like Phoebe, was too aggressive. Not that he objected to strong women. On the contrary, Rosso found it refreshing when women took the first step. It was more than that. There seemed to be no art to this kind of engagement. No playfulness. No cat and mouse.

Liz Taylor, by contrast, was more fetching. During their last conversation, Rosso was heartened that she had agreed to his revised rules of engagement.

> JR: Listen, I'm glad it's you, but we can't talk any more unless you tell me who you are.
> Liz: You don't like mystery?
> JR: I love mystery. I'm sick of nutcases. What's your name?
> Liz: Anne
> JR: Nice name.
> Liz: Thanks.

JR: Annie Oakley, Anne Boleyn, Anne Frank.
Liz: A sharpshooter, a decapitee, and a holocaust victim.
JR: Last name?
Liz: Farrell.

Their session was interrupted; at least this time "Liz," hereafter Anne, had not cut him off.

All of Rosso's professional expertise couldn't bring her back. Only, by now he was obsessed.

And, sight unseen, he was in love.

## 17

There comes a time in the life of anyone worth knowing that the gnawing inconsistencies, sustained by daily rituals and masked by fear, end up starved for real fare and begin to consume the soul. This was such a time for Charles.

He was living a lie.

On Charles's wedding day, Rosso, his best man, had attributed his friend's mood to last-minute nerves. The wedding guests, to whom Charles always remained a bit of a mystery, found their normally imperturbable friend endearingly human in this state. Rita sensed there might be more to it. As for Charles, he was consumed by the thought of Anne Farrell's suffering.

However much Charles loved Rita, which was a prodigious amount, he could not imagine life without Anne. At the same time, he had harbored no illusions; the roles of wife and mother had never suited her. Yet it was precisely Anne's self-knowledge and her independence from these everyday roles that made her company intoxicating. While most woman her age were marrying and raising families, Anne appreciated a man for who he *was*—precisely because she placed no traditional demands upon him.

In the course of his marriage to Rita, Charles had never been unfaithful. Yet Anne's hold on him lingered. He wondered about others who married. Did everyone step forward without complication? Or did some, like him, have a nagging conflict, an unresolved passion that went unseen—like the firefly's phosphorescence camouflaged by daylight.

Anne's illness had only made matters more complicated. On Charles's wedding day, this coincidence of love and loss began to hang over their marriage like an invisible fume. Both Charles and Rita were sickened by it, but only Charles knew its source. About Anne, he had told no one.

One night, near the end of November, Charles arrived home early after his case had been canceled. He handed his wife a bottle of champagne and a box of her favorite chocolate truffles. He kissed her, reminding her that it was the anniversary of the day he had proposed.

After that, Charles and Rita shared a rare moment of peace. He bathed his children, read to them, and put them to bed. Rita prepared their favorite dinner: grilled swordfish and risotto with artichoke. For the first time in a long while, the planets and stars had aligned themselves with what seemed like a singular resolve to address their needs.

After dinner, Charles started reading the *Scientific American* he had been trying to get to for months. "Did you know that a day is longer than a year on Mercury?"

"No, I didn't," Rita answered. She was absorbed in a history of the Habsburgs.

"A Mercury day is one hundred seventy-six earth days, but a Mercury year is eighty-eight earth days long."

"So what?" Rita offered.

"I'll tell you so what!" Charles replied excitedly. "That means that when someone is born on Mercury and turns two years old, he has barely lived a day."

Charles would not rest until he had charmed her intellect away from the vast number of entangling alliances created by the Austro-Hungarian Empire and lured it into outer space, light years away.

"I'm more interested in the Habsburgs," Rita said.

"The Habsburgs might be historically significant, but they're certainly not cosmic."

"How about Anne of Austria?"

"What about her?"

"Born in Spain. Queen of France. Unhappily married to Louis the Thirteenth. Retired to a convent after her son, Louis XIV assumed power."

"Central character in Dumas's *Three Musketeers*," Charles interrupted. "So what? She's dead!" He opened his palms and lifted his arms towards the sky. "But the universe," he cried, leaning over to kiss her. "Ah, the universe is infinite!"

"Do all the Annes end up dead?"

"What's that supposed to mean?"

"Anne Boleyn, Anne Frank."

Charles looked uncomfortable.

"What happened to Anne Farrell?"

In that instant, their spirited exchange collapsed.

"Is she thriving?" Rita persisted. "Did you save her?"

All of Charles's goodwill had dissolved. He felt betrayed by what he assumed to be Rita's foray into his personal files. Finally, he spoke, his voice grave and lifeless. "Why would you bring up something like this when we're having a moment's pleasure?"

"Because I'm sad."

"And you want me to be sad?"

"Yes."

Charles looked hurt. "Yet I try to shield you from sadness." What her husband said was true. He had never knowingly caused her any harm.

"It doesn't work," she said.

"What doesn't?"

"Trying to protect me."

"Why are you sad?"

She closed her book, looked up, and, in a tired voice, added, "Because I never had a chance."

Rita waited for Charles to respond, but he seemed paralyzed. Finally, Rita got up, and with a simple "Good night" made her way upstairs.

Charles sat lost in his thoughts. He was remembering a day nine years earlier when, for the last time, he had seen Anne healthy. He had taken her canoeing and had taught her how to paddle silently. Only the dragonfly's iridescent lace had caught the sun and made a noisy flash. They had banked on the other side of the lake, dragged their picnic provisions to an isolated spot and, by some unspoken consent, had abandoned the food. A red ladybug with black dots had parked on Anne's shirt. Charles had brushed it away, but Anne had caught his hand and led him to the button nearest her throat. Slowly, he had kissed her, soothed by the encouragement in her cool gray eyes. They had folded into each other with equal parts longing and piety.

## 18

Two weeks went by and Anne was still not on the calendar. When Lauren called again, Rosso agreed to meet with her—though only for coffee. As she spoke, Lauren's manner was intelligent and charming. He agreed to pick her up at work, after which Lauren would introduce him to her favorite diner.

Two days later, Rosso pulled into the parking lot of the New Day Spa Salon. The name alone stopped him. Though Lauren still claimed to love Emerson and Thoreau, her day job, she had explained, was running a health clinic. But this overdone Queen Anne-style house, with its wooden struts and gabled eaves, was no clinic and Lauren was clearly no "health professional."

*Fuhgeddaboudit*, Rosso muttered to himself, as he shifted into reverse. He completed his turn and headed for the exit.

A car blocked his path.

Rosso banged his horn.

One of the salon's employees emerged. She waved him out of his car and greeted Rosso with the enforced cheerfulness of Mao's China. Then she grabbed his car phone.

This dour six-footer from Minnesota introduced herself as

Inga. As Lauren's personal assistant, Inga claimed that her boss was mortified to be tied up so long with a client. "Lauren insists you enjoy a fifteen-minute massage," she said.

Inga pinned Rosso's arm behind his back and led him downstairs. There, in a basement refinished with dark Victorian panels and mirrors stood a tall man with curly hair. His paisley shirt, buttoned down to the only hair on his chest, along with hiphugger jeans flared slightly over his feet, made him look like something out of *Godspell* . Dozens of votive candles performed a riverdance to Celtic music and his image reflected infinitely.

"You must be Lawrence Franz," Rosso said.

However ridiculous he looked to Rosso, Franz was probably dangerous in that kinky, passive-aggressive, New-Age way. So, despite his loathing for cult figures, Rosso reminded himself that there would be no face to face, no mano a mano. No macho-macho man. He repeated to himself that he was a patient man, one who practiced non-violence and who had always admired Gandhi for his policy of passive resistance.

But when a barely audible Franz ordered Inga to "Put him on the massage table," Rosso completely lost it.

"Listen, you phony, sleazy, messianic mindfucker," Rosso said, "I could take this place with a loofah. So why don't you just release the women and let me out of here?"

Inga, who prided herself on her strength, harnessed all the discipline she possessed to resist decking Rosso. She looked towards her master for a signal. *Let me at him*, her entire being pleaded.

The signal never came.

Franz seemed preoccupied by a noise. Someone was banging on the front door. He waved Rosso away with the back of his hand, the unhurried gesture of a man both consumed by his own power and laden with contempt for others.

Inga escorted Rosso upstairs.

There, they were greeted by a policeman and one of his colleagues, a detective who held up his badge.

"We'd like to ask a few questions," he said.

Lauren emerged from the second floor stairwell. Her subtle makeup, French manicure, and designer clothes suggested that this ice queen had never kissed a frog, let alone set foot near Walden Pond.

The first officer introduced himself as Bob Caligari.

"What can I do for you?" Lauren smiled, glancing at Rosso.

Caligari turned to Rosso. "Are you James Rosso?"

Rosso extended his hand, "Yes, Officer." He gave Caligari a firm handshake. "I'll cooperate in any way I can."

"Good," the officer replied. "Detective Duncan and I will be taking you to the station for questioning."

*You've got be kidding me,* Rosso muttered to himself over and over again on the way to Wilton's police station.

The building was equipped with computer terminals, full-spectrum lighting, ficus plants, NO SMOKING lithographs, and the obligatory two-way mirror. Just as Rosso spotted the cappuccino machine, deeming it *ridiculous,* Duncan pulled out his case file.

"I'm allowed a phone call," Rosso said.

Duncan slammed the phone in front of him.

Rosso didn't know any criminal lawyers, so he called the hospital and had Charles paged. An OR nurse picked up. "I'm sorry, Dr. Dine is scrubbed and in surgery."

"It's an emergency."

"I'm sorry, but so's the retrohepatic injury to the I.V.C."

"Please tell him to call Jim at—"He looked up at Duncan, who reluctantly scribbled down the number. Rosso looked at the piece of paper and, on seeing the number, continued in a voice reduced to a whisper. "HOMicide 3522."

"HOMicide three, five, two, two?" she repeated loudly.

"That's right," Rosso winced.

In the background, he heard Charles call out, "I don't want cops calling my OR!"

"Dr. Dine should be closing soon," the nurse said. "He'll give you a call."

Rosso dropped the phone on the receiver and Duncan pulled it away.

"Want a *latte?*" he said, placing two crime scene photographs in front of Rosso.

"No."

"Do you know this woman?"

Phoebe had been beaten badly. The second shot was a closeup of her tongue; its tip had been cut off.

"Oh, God!" Rosso whispered.

"I asked you if you knew this woman"

"Yes," Rosso faltered. "I do."

"In what capacity?"

"We dated."

"Speak up!"

"I said, we dated."

"You dated?"

"Yes."

"And when it breaks off, you try to kill her."

"What!?"

"Then you leave her tongue in a soap dish just in case her last words happen to be Jim Rosso."

Duncan scanned a report as Rosso looked on in disbelief. "We've got you all over her apartment, in her files. She even left a letter on her computer and put a copy in her safety deposit box." He lit a cigarette. "Then we find you moving in on her best friend, Lauren."

"What are you talking about?"

"The lady at the beauty salon."

"I don't even know her," Rosso said.

He pictured Phoebe the last time he had seen her. She had

demanded to know who else he was dating. Clearly, she had been in danger.

"I've been set up," Rosso said.

"Who set you up?" Duncan asked.

"I'd like to make a phone call," Rosso said.

While waiting for Charles's call, Rosso refused to talk to Duncan. One hour into this silent vigil, the door opened. The station's Chief, Mark Talbot, introduced himself. Hope ran like a cool stream in Rosso's parched soul.

"Hey, Duncan. What have you got?"

"Preppie slimebucket. Attempted murder."

"Wrong man," Talbot interrupted. He grabbed Duncan's cigarette and snuffed it out. "You're really after Lawrence Franz." In an irritated tone, Talbot asked, "How long have you been here?"

"Five months."

"We've been after Franz for five years."

"Why can't you get him?" Rosso asked.

"No proof."

Talbot looked wearily at Rosso, as if to let him know what everybody on the squad knew: Duncan was a pudgy, pea-brained, fourth-generation policeman whose mannerisms had been picked up watching cop show reruns.

Two hours later, Charles arrived at the police station.

Not a word was uttered until Rosso had closed the door of Charles's Porsche.

"Thanks," Rosso said.

Charles started the engine. Rosso directed him past the police station and towards the salon where he had left his car. The moon was full. Its light covered the bleak November landscape with what looked like a thin coat of blue milk.

Rosso thought about Phoebe. The crime scene photos

flashed before him. Rosso rolled down the window and gasped for air.

"You've got to get this dating situation under control," Charles said.

"What's that supposed to mean?"

"It means that things have gotten out of hand. One woman left for dead, one tryst with a married Catholic, one ex-wife who's got you by the balls on account of a dog, and one complete fantasy who calls herself Elizabeth Taylor!" He shook his head in disapproval. "Where do you find these people?"

"The same goddamn place you did! Smartheart was your idea, remember!?"

"I never ended up a murder suspect."

"Welcome to modern single life."

"I don't think so."

"Yeah, well, I *know* so 'cause I'm living it." Rosso was suddenly angry for himself and for all single people. Charles had never had to deal with ex-boyfriends, ex-husbands, safe sex, or mindfuckers.

What's more, he had suggested that Rosso try Smartheart as matter-of-factly as he made his incisions.

"I can count on Sonny," Rosso said suddenly, when he had formulated what was bothering him.

"Who?"

"Sonny."

"Who the hell is Sonny?"

"He's my friend."

"Your exterminator?"

"Yes."

"Oh for Chrissakes! You've known him for a month."

"Yeah and I've known you for twenty years. I should have called *him*. I wouldn't have had to page, hold for five minutes, and wait three hours."

"Two."

"No, it was three!"

"Who cares?"

"I do! That's the point. When you're waiting, you know exactly how long you've been waiting. You've never waited for anyone, so how would you know!?"

"Oh, buck up! You sound like Rita!"

"Yeah, well, maybe she's on to something!"

"I'm tired of your bellyaching!"

"I'm tired of your surgery. I'm sick of your beeper going off every time we play golf, squash, or go to dinner."

"That's the job!"

"Fine. It sucks. Rita's a saint to put up with it. I don't have to."

"Fine!" Charles slammed on his brakes, almost running a red light. "You're the whiniest Navy man I've ever met."

"At least I served! You couldn't take Grenada with a slingshot!" The statement was both juvenile and preposterous. Rosso knew that Charles could have taken Grenada single-handedly. He was *The Bridge on the River Kwai* type; mentally and physically tough. The son of a bitch could do anything he set his mind to.

"Who showed up?" Charles asked. He tried to sound matter-of-fact, but he was wounded by Rosso's charges. Charles had always prided himself on his actions, which encoded his feelings. Even Rosso had to admit they were consistent for their follow through.

"You picked one date and it happened to work out," Rosso said.

"That's true. But if that date hadn't come along, I would have waited."

"You got lucky."

"Yes, but I can be alone."

"So you're saying that I can't?"

"You know you can't."

A surge of anger made Rosso ready to walk home.

"You're so fucking judgmental," he said. "I'm flawed. I'm divorced. I'm lonely. I want kids. *My own mother's a fucking newlywed!* You don't know what it's like out here."

"Bullshit."

"You don't have a clue."

Charles changed gears with a grinding noise that made Rosso glad his hands weren't free.

"I've had to patch up a man who was stabbed by his gay lover. I've had to extract nails from a pregnant woman's lower abdomen. Then, of course, there are people *so* far gone I can't do *anything*. So when I get a call from a best friend who needs to be bailed out, forgive me if I can't leave the OR!"

"Ah, but you can!" Rosso cried, matching Charles's tone and volume. "That's the *amazing* thing about free will!" Rosso added expansively. "You *chose* this life of eleventh-hour drama and you wrongly trivialize everyone else's. You think our struggles are mundane."

"They *are*."

"No, they're not. They're human!"

"It's your sloppy humanity that landed Phoebe on my operating table!"

Rosso was so stunned it doused his fury. He wanted to know how Phoebe was doing, but Charles's deranged driving suggested he was not finished. Rosso had never seen him so riled up.

"Maybe *you're* the one who doesn't know what it's like!" Charles cried. "*You* don't know what it's like to have a child die on you in the operating room. You don't know what it's like to face that child's parents. And you don't know what it's like to know that, however gut-wrenching it was, it would have been *worse*, vastly worse, if that child had survived."

They passed by the beach. The moon's reflection on the water made an inviting path, leading from the lip of the shore to the horizon. Rosso looked up. A single cloud extinguished the moon.

"I honestly don't know how you do it," Rosso said. The mere thought of losing a child, a spouse, a parent, a friend, or a dog produced unspeakable sorrow in Rosso.

He started to wonder what made the Phoebes of the world—those faithful, ductile, disciples who follow charismatic leaders willingly to their death. The very essence of this fanaticism violated Rosso's reverence for life. To complicate things further, Franz or one of his followers had tried to silence Phoebe—even cutting the tongue Franz thought would reveal secrets about him.

The sin of slander.

Phoebe's crime scene photos flashed before him. Rosso stuck his head out the window and threw up.

"You okay?" Charles asked quietly.

The car came to a halt in front of the salon.

"How is she?" Rosso asked.

"She'll make it."

Rosso opened the car door and signaled for Charles to wait. He started up his engine, then opened the window to thank his friend. "Do you want to stop by?" he asked.

"No. I've got to get home."

That night, Rita kept a lonely and restless vigil. She heard Charles come in but could not feel his presence. Occasionally, she would drop off to sleep, only to imagine Charles nursing a woman she had never met back to health. Worse still, when she woke up, she did not feel relieved; the dream did *not* feel implausible.

By 3 a.m., Rita was wide awake.

And Charles was gone.

# 19

Charles knocked on Rosso's door at 4 a.m. He handed a puzzled Rosso the cup of coffee he had bought at the 24-hour Royal Farms.

"I need to go away for a couple of days," he said.

"What?" Rosso glanced at his watch and opened the door wider, inviting Charles in.

"No, thanks."

"C'mon, it's freezing."

"I've got to round."

"So what are you doing here!?"

"I want you to tell Rita not to worry about me. Tell her I'll be back."

"Goddamn it, Charles! Why don't you tell her?"

"She's mad at me."

"Why? "

"She got wind of a former love."

"You've got to be kidding!"

"Long story."

"I swear to God, Charles. If you fuck up your marriage, I will personally chain you to a gurney and cut your balls off!"

"Reason enough to stay married."

"It's not funny! Are you fucking someone!?"

"No."

"Then who the hell are you going to see at 4 a.m., you inscrutable loon!?"

"I'll tell you when I get back."

"Tell me *now*."

"Can't. I'm only covered for seventy-two hours." He turned to leave and was halfway to his car when he called out, "Thank you, my friend. Call Rita. Don't forget."

Rosso locked the door and sat on the armchair closest to his fireplace. He stared at the single ember persisting amidst the ash and wondered why he pinned his hopes on the success of Charles and Rita's marriage.

He remembered the day Charles had summoned him to tell him about Rita.

On that February evening, nine years before, the snow had began to fall, dusting buildings, statues, and eyelashes alike. The street lights had glowed like ice balls the color of mango.

It was the last year of Charles's residency at New York Hospital. He had asked to meet Rosso about an important matter. He had suggested the Oak Bar at the Plaza Hotel. It was close to the hospital, and with its enormous windows, provided a magical setting for a blizzard.

The waiter had taken their order and Charles had stared out the window until his martini arrived. He told Rosso that he had met a woman named Rita through Smartheart and was sorting out the little he knew of her past. He was concerned about her previous boyfriend, "a goddamn monologist" named Jack. Rita had taken Charles to one of his performances.

"I'll bet his stuff sucked," Rosso had said, raising his glass.

"Actually, it was brilliant," Charles conceded. He had poked his index finger into the martini glass, secured the cocktail onion, and popped it into his mouth.

The waiter refilled the silver nut bowl. "Another round?" He signaled to Charles that a woman, two tables to his left, was looking at him.

"Please." Rosso had ordered another vodka, straight up.

"She must like doctors," the waiter added, noticing the scrubs under Charles's jacket.

Charles had turned towards the woman. Her cat-shaped eyes, the color of smoke; her delicate nose that finished off with a point; the straight bangs and shoulder-length hair which, along with her slender form, made him see her as a sophisticated woman, straight out of a Twenties photograph.

"She won't like me," Charles had said, smiling at the waiter. "I'm a surgeon."

"My opinion, since you asked for it, is that Rita's not in the bag, " Rosso had said.

"It's complex," Charles interrupted.

"No, it's *not*. Rita's still stuck on the thespian!"

Charles had turned his head towards the window. A man was helping a woman out of a horse-drawn carriage. He had brushed the snow off her hair and kissed her.

"Not necessarily."

"Yes, necessarily!"

"No, you see, she doesn't know what she wants."

"And you do?"

"Yes."

"So who gets the girl?"

"I do."

"What about Shakespeare?"

"He doesn't know what he wants either."

Rosso had hid his face in his hands and rubbed his eyes. It was close to midnight, though in the dark, mahogany bar, the crowd, transported by a haze of alcohol and the fairy-like scene outside, had lost all sense of time.

"It's very simple," Charles resumed. "When two people don't

know what they want, they don't end up together. When one person, who is convinced of what he wants, dates a woman who is unclear about what she wants, they often end up together."

"And why is that?" Rosso had sighed as the woman and her friend left.

"I have no idea. I just know that I'm going to win."

At two in the morning, they had left the Plaza. The sky was pink and the sharp, gray city lay frosted under two feet of snow.

Five hours after Charles left, the sun came up and Rosso was still in front of his fireplace, ruminating on the same subject.

By then, Charles had arrived in Newton, Massachusetts. Anne Farrell's hometown.

## 20

Thanks to Charles's visit, Rosso was up early. He waited until nine to call his mother. "I'm ready to meet Gus," he said, heartened that, in some matters, he was recovering his resolve.

"I was hoping you'd call," Flora said. He heard a muffled voice in the background. Then his mother asked, "How about today?"

Rosso was calm for most of the ride to New Jersey. In general, though, he wasn't himself. Pictures from the crime scene would pop up in his mind like grotesque roadsigns.

As he made his way to the Turnpike, Rosso remembered the late-night calls from single friends Doris had dubbed "non-essential." David Vimer had requested Charles's number after his date had punctured one of her implants. Artie, who had finally weaned himself away from prostitutes, had read in the early edition of the *Times* that the lawyer he was dating jumped to her death from the roof of her apartment building. Even Rita, who was not screwed up, reminded him about her dinner with a compulsive handwasher, followed by drinks with a real estate mogul who had had an ear job.

Dates from hell were the war stories of the single crowd, especially for those over thirty. Now that Rosso was in their shoes, he drew little comfort from these disturbing tales. The only reason he hadn't quit Smartheart was that it provided him a lifeline to Anne Farrell.

Rosso decided to give Smartheart one more month. If, at the end of January, he and Anne had still not met, he would accept the loss and welcome back his uneventful, yet dignified life as a Connecticut bachelor.

As Rosso neared the Montclair exit, he began to panic. Clammy hands, thumping heart, the whole deal. *What is your problem?* he asked himself. Get a grip, buck up, or as Yogi Doris used to say, *Take deep, cleansing breaths.*

As Rosso approached his mother's condo, he was diverted by the sight of some lunatic in a golf skirt practicing her putts. She was alone because it was freezing outside. Now, *that's* a fanatic, Rosso told himself, relieved that golfers like her made him look like a dilettante.

The closer he got to his mother's house, the odder the woman appeared. Until the woman became a man. A man wearing a kilt with a matching beret. Then, suddenly, his mother appeared, blowing on a set of bagpipes that squirmed like unruly pythons.

Rosso smiled. Touched and relieved by Gus and Flora's zany effort to diffuse tension, Rosso waved hello.

He pulled into the driveway and reached for the bouquet of yellow roses on the passenger seat. After he had stepped out of his car, Rosso handed his mother the flowers and kissed her.

"I thought you'd *never* get here! " Gus cried. "I'm not wearing pantyhose!"

"Nice legs," Rosso observed. He reached out to shake Gus's hand warmly.

Back in the house, Gus changed into his corduroys. He wore a gray cable sweater that Rosso could tell had been knitted by his mother. Only then did Rosso get the complete portrait of his mother's groom—about five foot nine, compact, vibrant, with irrepressible humor in his gaze. Very charming. Which was a good thing. Because Rosso believed that some elderly people fell into the Tiananmen Square category. You were in the tank, you despised yourself for even *thinking* about running them down. Then you stopped yourself, summoning up your nobler self, the one accountable to history and humanity. Other seniors were more like pandas. You wanted to hug them. Gus and his mother were clearly in the panda category.

The highpoint of his visit occurred during brunch. Sometime after the bagel with nova and before the scrambled eggs, Gus leaned over and whispered, "I hope your mother told you that we have a guest cottage in Boca. *On the golf course.*"

The morning proved so unexpectedly pleasant that Rosso surprised himself by not wanting to leave. In part because he dreaded calling Rita.

That afternoon, Rosso wondered if things might be looking up. He had received his first e-mail from Anne, who agreed to meet with him. As a result, Rosso scanned Smartheart's bios for the last time. He possessed the critical detachment of an angler who, to his amazement, had landed the loveliest mermaid.

**Smartheart, Inc. December Listing.**
Self-supporting CPA. Divorced with two wonderful children. Easygoing Wharton grad who loves the beach and trashy beach novels (Philadelphia).

Rosso punched up her bio.

FABIENNE MARSH

**Smartheart, Inc.**

**Name:** Ginny Price

**Occupation:** Accountant

**Schools:** Wharton School of Business, M.B.A.

**Address:** 92 St. David's Road, Swarthmore, Pennsylvania

**Age:** 41

**Description:** Brown hair, brown eyes

**Status:** Divorced

**Children:** Fifteen-year-old girl. Nine-year-old boy.

**Religion:** Episcopalian

**Hobbies (in order of importance):** Any movie with Leonardo DiCaprio.

**Favorite Books:** P.D. James mysteries; romance novels (the more insipid the better).

**What are you looking for in a companion?** Monogamy.

Dull. Very dull.

> **Smartheart Inc. December Listing.**
> Cornell graduate voted Woman of the Year and Chef of the Decade in Chicago Magazine. What a dish! (Chicago).

Rosso pulled up her bio.

**Smartheart, Inc.**

**Name:** Donna Witherspoon

**Occupation:** Chef

**Schools:** Cornell School of Hotel Management

**Address:** 20 Park Drive, Chicago, Illinois

**Age:** 33 Height: 5'2"

**Description:** Brown hair; blue eyes

**Status:** Single

**Children:** Tic-Toc

**Religion:** Tuscan Cuisine

**Hobbies (in order of importance):** Checking out the competition (eating out); swimming, and walking. Any tune by Pavarotti.

**Favorite Books:** The recipes of Ada Boni.

**What are you looking for in a companion?** A regular guy. No eating disorders.

Spirited, Rosso thought. Great, she loves to cook. The fact that *Chicago Magazine* had voted her Women of the Year meant absolutely nothing. Rosso was convinced that every year, in cities across America, grandmas *desperate* to marry off their grandchildren were hired by local publishers to pick the year's Most Eligible. The women were washed-up debutantes. The men were even worse —flatulent, flaccid mama's boys.

In the midst of his browsing, Rita called. Rosso had not forgotten his promise to Charles. He had been thinking of ways to broach the subject.

"This is awkward," Rosso began.

"Where is he?" Rita asked.

"He wanted me to tell you not to worry. That he'd be back."

"Fine." Rita said curtly.

Rosso could hear Tina crying in the background and he felt sorry for Rita. She was alone, on the kind of cold, gray Saturday that had parents scalping for tickets to the nearest dolphin show.

"I've got to go," she said.

Rosso offered to watch Rita's children for a few hours, but she declined. "It's not your problem," she said. When she fell silent, her despair was palpable.


That same afternoon, while her children were napping, Rita signed on. In the past few months, she had received dozens of responses to her "Elizabeth Taylor" bio, which had both surprised and flattered her. She had politely and sometimes playfully responded to queries—without ever soliciting any— and had never bothered to check who was contacting her. Her conversation with a man whose wife had run off with a Red Sock made her think of Rosso, but it was not until Rosso's birthday that her concern became more of a panic. At dinner that night, she had been terrified to learn of his interest in "Elizabeth Taylor." Rita had hoped that the matter would disappear. When Rosso persisted, however, she had agreed to meet with him which, in hindsight, struck her as an unnecessarily difficult and embarrassing way to put an end to the affair. After all, she could snuff herself out in the very medium she had introduced herself. That way, Rosso would never learn that he had been speaking to her all along.

Fear cinched Rita's heart when she called up the bio of a man who was one of three Jims she had chatted with. The address was familiar. On closer inspection, everything about the man was familiar.

**Smartheart Inc.**

**Name:** James Adams Rosso

**Occupation:** Computer Executive

**Schools:** Dartmouth

**Address:** 12 Hillside Lane, New Canaan, Connecticut

**Age:** 38. Height: 5'11"

**Description:** Brown hair, brown eyes.

**Status:** Divorced

**Children:** None

**Religion:** Fallen Catholic

**Hobbies (in order of importance):** Books, movies, most outdoor sports, and intelligent conversation.

**Favorite Books:** Churchill's *The Gathering Storm*; *Searching for Bobby Fisher*; *Catch-22*; and anything by C.S. Lewis.

**What are you looking for in a companion?** Happy, witty, fit, and attractive woman with brains and an irreverent sense of humor.

Rita could not take her eyes off the bio. When she did, she felt impure and somewhat unkind. Poor Rosso, she thought, I've disappointed him in the worst way. His earnest search; her stupid, casual flirtation. However unintentionally, she had trifled with his very soul. Minutes later, she found Rosso online.

JR: Thanks for the e-mail. Are we on?
Anne: There's something I have to tell you.
JR: Tell me when we meet.
Anne: I can't.
JR: Why?
Anne: I'm dead.

Rosso's cursor blinked, waiting to ferry his response.

JR: I've had days like that.
Anne: No. I'm really dead.

It occurred to Rosso that, given the recent events in his otherwise fairly uneventful life, it would be just his luck to be in pursuit of the most supremely unavailable person on the planet, the only member of Smartheart from the afterlife.

"I'm dead," Anne had written. Seconds later, Rosso put his hands on the keyboard.

JR: I don't care.

After signing off with Anne, Rosso called Rita to say that he was on his way over. At first, she refused.

"I'm not good company," she said.

"I don't care," Rosso insisted.

This echo from her conversation online would, under normal circumstances, have triggered another attempt on Rita's part to come clean, but on that bleak, wintry late afternoon, the more human need prevailed—the uncritical acceptance offered by a human being who was eager to comfort her.

When Rosso arrived, Rita looked drawn, forlorn, and bereft of all spirit.

Rosso did what any compassionate man would do and wrapped his arms around her.

# 21

On Sunday afternoon, Rosso stopped by the local video store to rent *Sunset Boulevard*. In the opening scene, the main character lay face down in a swimming pool, narrating an account of his own death. Impossible. Just as implausible as Anne speaking to him from the afterlife. Whoever she was, Rosso reasoned, she *had* to be alive.

He switched from his Bobby Orr video to the Classic Sports channel and back again. Doris was at a painting workshop, so he moped around with Rascal, who seemed to understand his feelings about Anne as well as his hope for Phoebe's well-being.

Ten minutes later, Mrs. Becker called. "A million!" she said. "I can now get you a million for your house. How does a *million* sound?"

Rosso was annoyed, but after he hung up, he started thinking about the house. In two years, he had replaced the boiler, repaired the roof, and rewired the house after an air conditioner had caused an electrical fire. Every knick-knack Doris had insisted was "period" had either pulled off in his hands or become a chewy for Rascal. The original wood floors creaked and closet space was at a premium because, Doris had told him, closets during the colonial period counted as an additional room and the King of England taxed them accordingly. So forget about tea, Rosso concluded, the revolution had been about closets. And Rosso had none. Rosso was beginning to tire of terms like "colonial" and "old world charm." They were real estate code for Money Pit.

Rascal dropped her rope at Rosso's feet. A few minutes into their tug, she broke loose and scampered upstairs like a high-stepping circus dog. She emerged from under the bed with a piece of paper between her teeth.

"Don't swallow that, Rascal! I'll get you a chewy." Rascal shoved her wet nose into his palm and dropped the piece of paper. "Good girl," Rosso said, exchanging it for a rawhide strip. He threw the paper into the trash and reached for the phone, but Rascal was fixated on the garbage can and started to scratch it. When someone knocked at the door at five o'clock, only then did Rascal offer an obligatory woof. "No, barking!" Rosso cried sternly. The week before, Doris had paid a trainer four hundred dollars to shut Rascal's yap.

While the dog resumed pawing the can, Rosso approached the door. From behind its glass panel, he could see Charles peering in. Despite the cold, he wore neither gloves nor hat.

"Thanks, friend," Charles said, as Rosso opened the door. He handed him a jug of maple syrup. "I'm on my way home."

"Are you going to tell me what's going on?"

"Yes, but not now." He seemed buoyant about matters unrelated to his trip. As if reading Rosso's mind, Charles added, "Don't worry about Phoebe," he winked. "I sent her home this morning."

As Rosso watched Charles walk towards his car, he was overcome with gratitude. How someone, *anyone*, could take a woman left for dead, resuscitate her, sew back her tongue, and restore her life was a godly act. That the person who had done so happened to be his friend was a source of intense pride.

Rosso held a single prayer for Phoebe—that she would repair her spirit with the same painstaking care hospital workers had employed to rebuild her body. At some point, Rosso knew he would have to say something to Phoebe—call her, write a note, something. Just thinking about it made him uncomfortable, but he knew it was the right thing to do.

In the midst of Rosso's reflection, Charles, who was conscious of leaving a bit too abruptly, turned back and asked cheerfully, "Had that date, yet?"

"No," Rosso replied, somewhat jarred by the intrusion.

"Why? "

"She was tired." However untrue, that was all Rosso was prepared to say.

"Tired!?" Charles persisted.

"Dead tired."

Charles shook his head in disapproval. "Dump her."

"I don't want to talk about it," Rosso said.

"Why not?"

"Because I reveal everything and you reveal nothing."

"Oh for Chrissakes! " Charles chided. "Did you at least get her name?"

"Yes!"

"Excellent! What is it?"

"Anne."

"Anne what?"

"Anne Farrell. "

"Anne Farrell!?" Charles cried softly.

"Anne Farrell," Rosso repeated.

Charles stared into the dark, immobilized.

"Do you know her?"

From inside the house came a deafening noise. "Hold on a second," Rosso said. He ran into the kitchen to see what mischief Rascal had caused. She had knocked over the plastic trash bin and was rummaging through its contents. Unlike

Rosso, Charles would have taken the time to clean it up then and there, but Rosso hated to keep people waiting. He rushed back to the door and, on seeing Charles walking towards his car, ran out.

"What's your problem!?" Rosso shouted.

Charles kept walking.

"Can't you even wait a *minute*!?"

"You said a second."

Rosso grabbed Charles's arm. "What's the matter with you!?"

Charles stopped, reached for his keys, and said, "If it's the Anne Farrell I know, you can give up on her."

"*Why*!?" Rosso cried.

"You'll just have to take my word for it." His resolute profile stayed fixed on his car.

"Stop acting like some fucking oracle! Tell me *why* and tell me *now*!"

Charles turned to face Rosso. "She was my patient," Charles said. That was all he would say. Then he got in his car and drove off.

Every bit of life seemed squeezed out of Rosso. He looked up. The sky was hard and finite; he felt locked inside a dark blue marble.

It was possible, of course, that Charles knew another Anne Farrell, but in his gut, Rosso did not think so. He saw it as typical of his forays into the single world. Just as Rosso thought he had broken new ground, all roads led to Charles, or to the fact that everyone knew someone who knew Charles, or, worse still, that a prospective date knew people Rosso knew. And this whole messy pre-history of social relations sometimes pulled people apart before they had even met, as fiercely and inexorably as an undertow.

An unmarried, urban, Smartheart of forty was, for some reason— *didn't matter what*—either a loner, unbelievably picky (if female), a functioning sociopath or serial dater (if male), or, based on the nocturnal confessions Rosso had been privy to during his brief tenure as a Smartheart dater, the unfortunate victim of child abuse, gender confusion, or the unconscious possessor of some untapped rage. The problem was they all wanted, or *thought* they wanted, a mate.

It dawned on Rosso that nice guy after nice guy—or schmuck after schmuck—who had preceded Rosso had caused many of the women he was dating to cultivate a dater's radar, to be suspicious of the slightest compliment, to react to the best-intentioned remark, or to dismiss, without appeal, any romantic possibility on the basis of traits which, Rosso knew for a fact, could be changed—bad ties, unshined shoes, oversized glasses, uncapped toothpaste, sniffling through dinner, clothes left in piles, the jangling of pocket change, or a death grip on the television's remote control. If anything, the most intractable irritants in the healthiest relationships often became a source of humor. Too sensitive a radar by too seasoned a dater turned an isolated example of human frailty into the behavioral equivalent of some Titanic-sinking iceberg; thus, Rosso decided, too much information, analysis, and speculation produced overreactions and bad calls.

For this perception, Rosso realized he was more experienced than all his savvy Smarthearts. He suddenly took comfort in the fact that those unacquainted with frailty and discord, and those who lacked imagination, patience, humor, and common sense, should probably not be married in the first place.

All this self-approbation was well and good, especially for a divorcé who had been laboring unconsciously under the assumption that his failed marriage gave never-married daters the right-of-way regarding judgments of the heart. It even left Rosso feeling more charitable towards Charles, who had said that he was incapable of being alone. With regard to Rosso's current circumstances, being alone *was* preferable.

With one vexing exception.

For Rosso, there remained a single, blinding, heart-searing desire for which he was prepared to comb the beaches, search the landing grounds, scour the fields, man the streets, and, to further paraphrase his beloved Churchill, *never surrender* until he could logically, calmly, and with any degree of certainty, dismiss Anne Farrell as a romantic possibility.

Once inside his house, Rosso bent over to clean the mess Rascal had made. His movements were slow and deliberate, keeping tempo with the thunderous phrases still looping in his head.

He glanced at his wall calendar. At the end of January, Future Systems was hosting a firewall seminar at the Ritz-Carlton in Boston. Rosso had always considered the meeting optional, but since Anne had yet to set a date, he decided to tell her that he would be in her neck of the woods. If she could not meet with him, for whatever reason, then he would blow her off.

Rascal bounded in carrying the piece of paper she had retrieved from the trash and dropped it on Rosso's thigh. It was a card. A business card. Rosso turned it over.

**Ronny Spiro**
Pest Control
*All species including human.*
*Attitudes are the Real Disability*

## 22

Five years after Sonny the ratter and his wife, Lourdes, had divorced, the one thing that continued to keep them civil towards each other was their children. Outside this mutual love for their boys, Sonny was not sure how he stood. Since Lourdes was the only contact he had at St. John's Hospital, he was about to find out.

"I need a favor, " he said. The Emergency Room sounded fairly slow; perhaps he stood a chance.

"What is it?"

"I need information on a former patient."

"Who's the doctor?"

"I can't say."

"It'll be on the discharge."

"I still can't say."

"How are the boys?"

"Diego made the soccer team. Miguel was voted class treasurer. What's the patient's name?"

"Anne Farrell."

He heard Lourdes clicking on a computer keyboard. She was

fast. She was good. He had always been told that St. John's was lucky to have her as an ER clerk.

"Transferred out of the SICU on April 30th. Dr. Dine signed her discharge papers on May 10th, 1995."

"Where did she go?"

"Newton, Mass."

"Who picked her up?"

"Her parents."

"Is she alive?"

"She was then."

"What about now?"

"I don't know."

Sonny thanked her and promised he would never reveal her as a source. He felt obligated to make small talk, but since Lourdes 's boyfriend was responsible for Sonny's current gastro-intestinal upset, it was with considerable discomfort that Sonny asked, "How's Mario?"

"*Una mierda.* I kicked him out," she snapped. Because she had learned not to give Sonny any hope of reconciliation, she added, barely pausing to breathe, "You're a good man, but if you were the last man on earth, I still wouldn't want to get back together."

For the next couple of hours, a somewhat bruised Sonny busied himself with street maps of Anne's neighborhood. He was thankful to have a client who was both generous and who appreciated his work.

Two days later, Rosso noticed an unnerving item on the Smartheart homepage. Anne's membership number appeared on the "List of Members not Renewing." Those people, he mused, who had either found love or had given up. He wondered if it was Anne's way of losing his scent. If so, why had she agreed to meet with him? Rosso barely knew the woman, yet he felt rejected. Anne's spirit had carried him through these lonely, wifeless, date-fearing, Franz-infested and, until recently, dogless months. Despite the infernal disconnections, the elusive appointments and, most bizarre, Anne's apparent link to Charles, the hope of meeting this refreshingly original woman had kept Rosso's innermost being patient and cheerful.

In his office later that day, Rosso looked at the week of January fourteenth on his calendar. Because the matter had been weighing on him, he decided to call Phoebe. The whole thing felt so awkward—as if their brief union had overstayed its welcome, even *before* the savage turn of events.

When Phoebe picked up on the fourth ring, Rosso was content to hear her speak. The injury to her tongue, she said, was healing; so were the scars on her face. When Rosso offered a get well visit, she started to cry, saying that she would ask her therapist. One hour later, Phoebe called to decline the visit, leaving Rosso embarrassed by the enormity of his relief.

Returning to his calendar, Rosso called his mother and, to her delight, invited himself to Boca for Christmas. He could tell that Gus was all bag, but Rosso nonetheless looked forward to playing golf with him. As for January, Rosso booked a flight to Boston on the nineteenth. He pulled out a golf club, which doubled as a pen in the deskset his sister had given him, and circled the days he could meet Anne for dinner. Saturday the twentieth looked best. He e-mailed Anne to propose the date. After that, he reached for his miniature golf ball, unclipped the business cards it held, and putted a hole-in-one on the miniature green. When he tried to jam the cards back, only one refused to conform.

It was partly torn with a toothmark punched through its zip code. Rosso smiled on recalling his Lab's antics, then he picked up the phone. Rascal had been right; there was only one man qualified to track down Anne Farrell.

Rosso punched his speed dial. "What have you got?" he asked Sonny.

"She's alive and lives in Newton, Massachusetts."

"I thought she was in Boston."

"Newton's eight miles from Boston. I know it's her."

Later that afternoon, Sonny arrived in Rosso's office, delivering maps. He popped a CD ROM into Rosso's computer and pointed to a small *cul de sac* where he suspected Anne lived.

"15 Elkhurst. Do you want me to scout the location?"

Sonny waited for a reply, but his normally expressive client stared sullenly at the map.

Newton, Sonny went on to explain, was first settled in 1630, incorporated as Cambridge Village in 1688, and was renamed Newton in 1873, when the city received its Charter. Today, the population was approaching one hundred thousand and it was a nice town, with distinctive neighborhoods.

Then Sonny printed out the map.

Rosso's primary concern was whether Anne Farrell checked out. Otherwise, he would just be making a fool of himself in Boston.

"Is something wrong?" Sonny asked.

"Yes."

"What?"

Rosso sighed. "I'm chasing a butterfly."

"Why do you say that?"

"She doesn't want to be caught."

"Did she cancel on you?"

"She hasn't confirmed, but for all I know, she could be a three hundred-pound disgruntled English professor who hates men and serves God by trapping them online."

Sonny abandoned his customary professionalism and took on the manner of a much-needed coach. "This is the closest you've gotten," he said. "I'd hate to see you give up now."

Rosso was closing down the windows on his computer when his message icon started to blink.

"It's her," Sonny said.
"No, it's not."

An impatient Sonny reached past Rosso with his disfigured arm and poked up the message.

Does 7:30 in the lobby of the Ritz suit you?

## 23

On mornings after an argument, the day has a way of staring back—as if it has become bolder than you and will control not only that morning but all mornings and, perhaps, all evenings for the rest of your life. At least, that's how Rita saw it. After Charles's absence, with the exception of her brief trip home, she found herself engaged in simple tasks. She spent the better part of two days with her son's small toy farm. There was something cheerful and purifying about teaching Daniel animal sounds.

Daniel's pediatrician, Dr. Connor, was concerned that Daniel only had six words—and Rita had cooked the numbers by counting quack-quack as two. He recommended that Daniel be tested. At first, Rita protested, "He's not even two!" Since the waiting list was months long, she thought the prudent thing would be to make the appointment; it would both placate the pediatrician and buy her son time. On the eve of the evaluation, two weeks before Daniel turned two, Rita had planned to discuss the matter with Charles, but they had argued and he had left. While Charles was on his way to see Anne Farrell, Rita sat in a small room with Daniel and a neuro-developmental pediatrician, answering dozens of questions for the better part of two hours: Does he obey two-step commands? Can he tell you what dogs, cows, and pigs say? How many body parts can he identify?

Rita wondered why she had subjected her beloved son to all this. He was trying to distract himself by flipping the light switch. When that was discouraged, he lay on his belly, staring at the wheels of a truck. After the evaluation, they sent her off on a dark, rainy night with a diagnosis of "mild autism."

When she arrived home, Rita was so shaken that she overpaid the sitter by twenty dollars. Then she tucked her son in bed, gave her daughter a bottle, and searched the web for anything relating to the brain disorder that has captivated people's imaginations for centuries. By morning, she had read every scrap of information put out by The National Institutes of Health and other respected sources. She was spent, emotionally and physically. There was nothing "mild" about autism.

The hours that Charles was away were unendurable, not just because of her doubts about their marriage, but also because she worried about her son.

The day after the appointment, Dr. Conner called to ask that Daniel see a neurologist.

Rita hung up the phone and started to cry. She pictured her son's life: he would never marry; he would live alone; he would always be lost in his own fantasies. His sister, Tina, would have to care for Danny after she and Charles were gone.

It was to this unhinged world that Charles returned. Rita gave him the essential details, said that she had agonized over her decision, but concluded that Daniel should not be tested further. To her surprise, Charles smiled, sat down, and, despite her initial resistance, held her as if she was the person on earth he held most dear and said, "Good for you, honey."

"You don't even know what happened."

"I trust your judgment completely."

"These have been the worst two days of my entire life."

Charles stroked his wife's hair and ignored the phone when it rang. Fifteen minutes later, he said gently, "May I guess what happened?"

"Yes," Rita said.

"You asked for speech and they gave you a comprehensive exam because, secretly, Dr. Connor suspected that Daniel's speech delay was linked to something more serious."

She peeked out from under his arm.

"One of the doctors was a neurologist."

She nodded.

"He asked you what Danny loved, and because you were proud that he was exhibiting typical male toddler behavior, you boasted that he loved ceiling fans, light switches, VCRs, and boom boxes."

"That's right."

"Bingo," Charles said.

"What do you mean?"

"I mean he had everything he needed to make a diagnosis. "

"It's my fault."

"On the contrary. The man's an idiot with no instincts about children."

Underlying Charles's singular opinion was the larger truth that all surgeons hated medical doctors. "Neurologists test for a million things, causing great discomfort to a child and incalculable misery to a parent, then they say, it's probably not x, y, or z, but we think it might be q. In Danny's case, they took VCR's, trucks, ceiling fans, and light switches—"

"But all boys his age love that stuff—"

"Exactly. But what you call fascinations, they call fixations. Then the numbskull lumped speech delay with fixations, or stereotypies. So after asking your questions for hours and watching Danny out of the corner of his eye for a few *minutes*, he came up with a probable diagnosis of autism."

"That's it!"

"Which is why I didn't go into medicine. We don't tell people they *might* have cancer, liver disease, a bowel obstruction, or anything else. They do or they don't."

Rita closed her eyes. Her son's mischievous smile filled her palpebral screen. She pictured him taking things apart, trying to put them back together. "He's an engineer," she whispered. When she opened her eyes, it was Charles who was blinking back tears.

"What's the matter?" she asked.

"I honestly can't believe that anybody, let alone a doctor who specializes in children, would not and could not take the time to understand so intriguing a little boy."

Rita admired the loyalty, respect, and love that Charles held for his son. *All* his loves, her included, were profound and life-changing. Which is why, with regard to Anne, matters were more complex than they appeared. In her heart, Rita knew that she could never despise anyone Charles held dear. His taste in people was inspiring.

Charles went to bed without discussing where he had been and why. "I know you need to know certain things," he said. "In time, you will. Until then, please trust me. I love you." Charles kissed Rita with an intensity that stirred up a passion held in reserve for him, and only him.

## 24

On the twentieth of January, Rosso glanced at the clock in the lobby of the Ritz-Carlton. Seven forty. Anne was ten minutes late. He thumbed through a copy of *The Boston Globe*, waved at one of his colleagues, stepped in and out of the bar, and walked out to Arlington Street, where a blast of cold air gave him the tonic he needed to begin his idiosyncratic cycle of waiting all over again.

Back in the lobby, he checked the time; seven fifty. Seven fifty-five according to Rosso's watch. He called Doris to check in on Rascal, since she had just been neutered, and contemplated the irony. How is it that you get the wife you want only when she's your ex? After he hung up, he noted the time: Anne was now running twenty-five minutes late. He would give her ten more minutes.

He had just sat down and buried himself in a copy of *The Atlantic* when Bob Hersh stepped out of the elevator. A few seconds later, Hersh was standing over him, appearing more animated than usual, with a dimple Rosso had never seen before dancing on his left cheek.

"Don't make plans for breakfast," Hersh said. "I've got a surprise for you."

Then, to Rosso's horror, Hersh sat down to chat.

"Are you dating?" he whispered.

Rosso did not want to talk about it.

"I'm not interested in your kissie-kissie stories," Hersh persisted. "I'm asking on behalf of my daughter, Lily." His last words were "I won't keep you" but he went on to say that he could not stand the guys Lily was meeting.

"That's would be a difficult situation, sir," Rosso said. He was distracted by an elegant woman in a cashmere coat who had just come in. He caught her eye. Could it be? Beautiful face, Elizabeth Taylor's coloring. His mind raced. She was half an hour late. Tardiness was *not* good, Rosso reminded himself, but so what? He had just decided that they could work it out when the woman greeted a shriveled old codger who emerged from the Ritz's annual smoker's dinner with a cigar in one hand and a cognac in the other.

Even Hersh noticed. "How does a ruin like him land a goddess like her?" he asked, making way for the woman to pass. Without waiting for an answer, he started to blather about Lily. "She went to Williams," he explained. "Too smart for her own good. I'm worried she'll never marry. Says she doesn't care." He turned to Rosso. "Are you listening?"

"Maybe she doesn't care," Rosso offered, disgusted by the sight of the woman and her septuagenarian sugar daddy stepping into the elevator.

"I need grandchildren, goddamnit! Who am I gonna hunt with in my old age!? My luck, she'll give me a bunch of girls."

"Nothing the matter with girls, sir. " Rosso sighed.

"If they grow up to be smarty pants like her, there is." He glanced at Rosso. "Oh c'mon, Rosso! Men don't want to come home to a woman from MENSA. They want a drink, some gruel, and *above* all, *no yackety-yack*! I've got a brainy daughter who refuses to cook, doesn't drink, and has a mouth that never quits. How's a girl like that going to get married?"

*The same way you did, motor mouth!* Rosso thought to himself. He looked at the clock. Five more minutes. That's all Rosso was prepared to give her.

Hersh whipped out a laminated photo of his daughter which, he said, had been taken a few years earlier and handed it to Rosso. Pigtails, braces, and a pimple the size of blueberry. "Isn't she gorgeous? " he asked.

Rosso choked back an involuntary laugh, squeezing it into the more socially acceptable form of a cough. "You love her very much, " Rosso said. He coughed and coughed until the dam of his emotions broke, unleashing a torrent of hysterical laughter.

"What's so funny?" Hersh asked.

"I'm sorry, sir," Rosso said, then sputtered and howled some more.

The concierge hurried over. "Is something the matter, sir?" Before he knew it, what seemed like the Ritz's entire staff converged with the urgency of a SWAT team.

Rosso kept on heeing and hawing, like the ass he now knew himself to be. It struck him as ridiculous that Hersh was seeking advice for his beloved though butt-ugly daughter from a divorced loser who was in the process of being stood up.

Rosso saw Hersh dab his eyes with a gun rag he had retrieved from his briefcase. "What's the matter?" he asked.

"My wife died three years ago," he said, yanking his daughter's picture out of Rosso's hand. "Lily's my whole world."

The SWAT team disbanded, presumably because crying was routine; only laughter was subversive.

Five minutes after Hersh left, Rosso was kicking himself. *Look at yourself*, he thought, catching his reflection in a mirror next to the concierge, *You're looking at an asshole*. He took a final look at the clock in the lobby. He had waited a full hour. Anne was still a no-show.

She's history, he told himself. Push on.

He decided to bag the conference and go home.

The next morning, Rosso found Hersh on the fifteenth floor, finishing his first client breakfast in the club lounge. Hersh waved him over, spotted his garment bag, and asked, "Where do you think you're going?"

"Home," Rosso said decisively. "But first I want to apologize for last night. Nervous laughter, sir. I was stood up."

"Sorry to hear that, but you're still coming with me. The car's out front. This is your lucky day."

"It really isn't," Rosso said. He had not slept all night and he wanted to go home. The last thing he needed was to have breakfast with Hersh, let alone drive to an undisclosed location. He was hoping that Hersh's first breakfast date would stay, but the man, who looked relieved to see Rosso, stood up and shook his hand as vigorously as if he had just won the Publisher's Clearinghouse Sweepstakes. Then he left.

"Oh, come on, Jim! A good-looking guy like you can *always* get another woman, but there's only one Bobby Orr, and *goddamn it if we're not having lunch with him!*"

"Bobby Orr?" Rosso asked. His voiced dropped in reverence, soft as a church-pew whisper.

Much as he was devastated by Anne's no-show, Rosso righted himself and reshuffled his priorities. *Bobby* Orr!?—the hockey player from Parry Sound Ontario who had played for the Boston Bruins and the Chicago Blackhawks. Bobby *Orr*? The first defenseman ever to win a scoring title—*twice!* Bobby, the blueliner of genius who backhanded a goal against Kenny Dryden from behind the goal line in the 1971 playoffs; Bobby, the skater of speed and grace, who scored the last goal in overtime during the 1970 Stanley Cup Finals!

Robert Gordon Orr was the most valuable member in Rosso's Hall of Fame, which included Jean Beliveau, Yvan (The Roadrunner) Cournoyer, Gordy Howe, and Maurice (The

Rocket) Richard—*any* of whom he would be honored to have lunch with. But Bobby Orr! Truly the greatest player ever to lace a pair of skates.

"Don't disappoint me," Hersh growled. "I set this up months ago."

# 25

Rita's discovery of the last two cards in Charles's file proved ghoulish.

*Transferred to SICU two days ago.*
*Remains responsive only to painful stimuli.*
*On full ventilatory support.*
*Hermodynamically stable; however, this morning, creatinine bumped to 3.5.*
*Bilirubin up to 7 with elevated liver enzymes.*

Then, at the very edge of the last card, recorded in a shaky hand, she read words that chilled her.

*April 22, 1995: Four organ systems failing.*
*Chance of survival nil.*

April 22, 1995 had been their wedding day.

By all accounts, it had been a spectacular one, beginning with rain and giving way to dappled sunshine, varnished grass, hard-fisted peonies, and water drops that either danced on telephone wires or sparkled like diamonds in an endless cache of spider webs. Everything alive seemed touched by the same fearless beauty. Only Charles had appeared subdued. To Rita, it was now clear why.

As for Rita's husband, he was presently in a bit of a quandary himself. The last time he had seen Rosso, Charles had tried to piece together how his friend could possibly have met Anne Farrell. She had never been a Smartheart subscriber, so, he wondered, what was the link?

Since his wife had recently learned about Anne from his files, Charles decided that she was the only possible link between Anne and Rosso. But how? And why? Charles began to wonder, *what was Rita up to?* The rub was that, just now, it was not in his interest to find out, for it would only mean more disclosures on his part.

In the meantime, Rita had been won over by Charles's response to their son's faulty diagnosis. For the first time in weeks, peace had come over her like a slow, sweet ether. She felt like a child who had been reassured that her darkest nightmares had no bearing on the day.

During this period, it had occurred to Rita, with joy, resolve, and characteristic pluck, that the best way to end matters with Rosso was to quit Smartheart and to come clean with Rosso before Charles got wind of anything. She did so with a modicum of chagrin. Her conversations had both stimulated her and had given her a perverse sense of freedom—at no one's expense until now. Now that Rita was no longer innocent; that is, now that she knew she was speaking with Rosso, she asked herself why she had not cut things off. The only thing that made sense was that, given her absolute shock and the sense of betrayal she had felt about her husband's affair with Anne, she had fought deceit with deceit in some primal struggle for survival.

At the same time, in some strange act of self-delusion, Rita had told herself that she was doing Charles a favor by keeping Anne alive. Her husband's private file had revealed that many of his patients, who were very sick to begin with, had died. She was convinced that Charles kept the file as a *memento mori*, to remind himself that, even though modern surgery could perform miracles, he was not God. Charles's own mother had died waiting for a kidney. She now believed her husband had devoted his life to bringing his mother and countless others back.

One day, after Charles had left for the hospital, and before her children were awake, Rita decided to put the entire Smartheart episode behind her by confronting the one item in Charles's file which, up until now, she had not had the nerve to pursue: the small, brown paper bag with the perfectly-drawn heart. Its very existence made Rosso's revelation on the golf course months before seem counterfeit, uninformed, or both.

At first, the bag's contents seemed harmless enough. What looked like a wad of crushed paper had once served as a napkin. On closer inspection, Rita saw that it had been folded into an airplane. A telephone number appeared on the wing, along with the puzzling words "You never know."

Rita wondered. Had the first sparks between Anne and Charles flown by way of this airborne calling card? She decided it was so and suddenly this small fossil of emotion, lacking weight and volume but replete with significance, left Rita entirely undone. In that instant, everything Charles had not been prepared to discuss became the sum total of what she wanted to know. How had Anne and Charles met? How had she become his patient? Just how intimate had they been? And what had happened to her?

The only person she could turn to was Rosso. But just how much did Rosso know? Besides, Rosso was first and foremost Charles's friend. She knew men to be proprietary on matters of the heart, but she also knew Charles to be extremely private. It was possible that Rosso didn't know about Anne and Charles—especially since Rita suspected that Rosso never would have misled her about her husband's feelings towards her. What's more, how could she bring up Anne Farrell when poor Rosso was on a quest of his own—in search of an Anne Farrell whose identity Rita had appropriated in an unbecoming moment of mischief?

Over the past few weeks, things had only become more complex as Rita's concerns about her son had mounted. That said, she blamed herself for lacking resolve. Rosso still thought that Anne Farrell was meeting him for a drink at the Ritz-Carlton on the twentieth of January because, on a day she had felt trapped, on a day she had possessed so little hope, Rita had fantasized about leaving, just leaving. When Rosso's e-mail proposing the twentieth had come in at the precise moment her feelings were at their peak, she had been crazy enough to agree—and *flee*, electronically—simply by pressing "Reply." Worse still, when she had come to her senses, she had not possessed the presence of mind to cancel.

A stab of fear overtook her as she flipped through her date book. For Rita, the days had melted together, without distinction—yet in the world outside, it was now, incontrovertibly, the twenty-second of January. She pictured Rosso standing in the lobby of the Ritz-Carlton, eyes trained on the door. What a *mess*, she shuddered.

## 26

On the way to Bobby Orr's house, the driver got lost. At first Rosso was oblivious; he was too busy composing questions for Bobby and dreaming up ways to play golf with him. But minutes later, Rosso found himself flinching at the street names. Chestnut, Walnut, Cherry. According to Sonny's maps, they were passing through Anne Farrell's neighborhood.

"What's the matter, Jim?" Hersh asked. "You're wound tighter than a working bird dog."

"Nothing, sir."

Rosso felt the sweat beading up on his brow and loosened his necktie.

Hersh looked over at Rosso. "Stop the car, driver." Hersh opened the door and kicked him out. "Get some air. I'll call Bobby while the driver checks the map."

At ten o'clock in the morning, Rosso found himself standing in front of 15 Elkhurst—a small ranch made of red brick and white wood with black shutters. The house was impeccably maintained with lace curtains on the living room windows. A few yards away, a sheer, nylon curtain wafted out of a large French window, as if to beckon the world in.

By looking at the house, Rosso knew that Charles had told him the truth. You could look at a house and know that a sick person lived there. Rosso imagined a young person who was probably being looked after by her parents; he guessed that her family's wealth had been siphoned by medical bills. Standing there, Rosso understood why Anne's imaginative life inversely corresponded to the physical realities of her life. Suffused with sadness, Rosso decided to leave well enough alone and headed back to the car.

A few moments later, he heard a woman's voice. "May I help you?"

Rosso turned towards the voice. The woman was in her early thirties, dressed in slimfit khakis, a white mock turtleneck, and a red down vest.

"May I help you?" she repeated.

Rosso smiled. Her bright eyes invited a response. After some hesitation, he spoke. "Anne?" he asked quietly, then clearing his throat and gaining confidence, he asked again, "Are you Anne Farrell?"

"No," she smiled. "I'm her sister Ruth. Is Anne expecting you?" Rosso was paralyzed. He cursed himself for not respecting his first instinct. Suddenly, he wanted to escape as stealthily as he had arrived—unobserved, unaccounted for, like a cipher. Instead, to justify his intrusion, and without thinking, Rosso blurted out that he was a friend of Charles Dine's.

"Any friend of Dr. Dine's is a friend of ours," Ruth said warmly, walking down the driveway to greet him. "Won't you come in?"

Rosso glanced toward the car and saw Hersh on the car phone. Hersh, who had come to expect odd happenings from Rosso, waved him on. "Go ahead," he shouted. "We're meeting Bobby at his favorite restaurant. You've got time!"

Rosso's steps grew heavier and more reluctant, as if bound by the leaden inevitability of a bad dream. He knew that Ruth would lead him to the room with the open window. Once inside, he expected to see a computer—the mainstay of Anne's emotional life. Instead, they passed a kitchen which smelled of boiled cauliflower and continued down a hallway whose gray carpet had no pile. When they could go no further, Ruth stepped into a small, neat room the color of vanilla and flooded with light. It was so bright that, at first, Rosso did not see the hospital bed. Nor did he notice the grotesque scar from the tracheotomy tube. Minutes later, the knobby veins from dialysis appeared on her arms.

A woman stood up, unsteady on her feet. "What a surprise," she smiled. "It's been a while, but Charles speaks of you constantly." Her face was drawn, but that of an angel's—kind, serene, and beautiful.

Her cat-shaped eyes, her delicate features.

Rosso's brain swarmed to place the face.

He remembered the woman smiling in Charles's direction.

He saw Charles scribbling something on his napkin. He saw Charles make an airplane and toss it towards the woman as Rosso, along with those in the plane's path, had watched it glide to a stop in front of her champagne glass.

"Nice shot," she had mouthed.

Charles had smiled broadly, even uttering, "Thanks."

"I've never seen you like this!" Rosso had exclaimed.

Outside, the snow had fallen thick as feathers, casting a white glow back into the otherwise dark bar. The woman had unfolded the plane and frowned.

"What did you write?" Rosso had asked.

"I told her I was taken," Charles had said.

A second plane had hit Charles in the chest and landed on his lap. Rosso had peered over his friend's shoulder. On the wing, the woman had written her phone number, along with the words "You never know." When Charles and Rosso looked up, she was laughing at something her girlfriend had said and buttoning her coat.

Rosso's face drained of all color, then burned with shame as it occurred to him that the woman from the Oak Bar, nine years before, was Anne Farrell.

"He told you he was taken," Rosso whispered.

"He was," Anne said. "He still is."

She watched Rosso closely, pitying his confused state. "Isn't life absurd?" she asked gently.

Just then, Hersh's vigorous knock at the door seemed to shake the entire house.

## 27

Day one, he canceled his Smartheart membership. Day two, he took a six-mile run. The day after that, he wrote a long thank you letter to Bobby Orr. And finally, at the end of the week, he called his Navy buddy at the FBI. Rosso was convinced he had finally gathered enough evidence to put Franz in the slammer.

"Let's have a lookee-see," Mike had said with the relaxed confidence of a professional at the top of his game.

After arranging a drop-off time with Mike, Rosso called Doris because he missed Rascal. He was thinking about filing for custody. When a man answered the phone, Rosso was confused until he recognized the voice as that of Doris's father, Peter Bonno, Senior. Since he and Pete had always been on good terms, Rosso confessed his relief.

"I thought you were the ball player."

"I gather he's no longer on first," Pete said.

"Say, Jim?"

"Yes?"

"Are you and Doris divorced yet?"

"Yes, we are."

"Too bad."

When Doris finally got on the line, she was exuberant. She had secured her real estate license, sold her first house, and was celebrating with her new boyfriend, a pro-golfer.

"A golfer!?" You've got to be kidding me."

"He's been very good to Rascal."

"Golf! Labs!? All the things you used to hate me for."

"You've taught me a lot, Jim."

Great, Rosso thought. Doris liked Labs, golf, and children. Maybe she had never known *what* she wanted. Maybe she had discovered that, all along, she wanted what her girlfriends wanted—the very things Rosso had wanted. Yet, if they had arrived at the same place, then why hadn't they been able to patch things up?

It occurred to Rosso that, in the course of their marriage, Rosso had not changed much but Doris had turned thirty, a turbulent age marked by his wife's first summing up. During her twenties, Doris had gone along unthinkingly, until they had moved to the suburbs. Then, suddenly, the very assumptions she had always taken for granted—marriage, children, and her life as a painter—fell apart the minute she began to examine each one. During this period, Rosso was roadkill to the engine of his wife's newly emerging desires. The unspoken contract by which he and Doris had come together suddenly needed revising.

She didn't want to be the artist anymore.

Looking back, Rosso realized that he had wanted an artist and that Doris had wanted someone to let her be an artist. But, though she had an artist's affect, and surrounded herself with people who acted and dressed the part, Rosso suspected that, deep down, despite her Prix de Rome, Doris knew she had no exceptional talent.

She had become the painterly equivalent of the waitress who calls herself an actor, or the model who is *really* a painter, or the advertising executive who is *really* a director, or the wedding singer who has been pursuing a record deal for over a decade. In the course of her marriage, Doris had come to see herself as an artist (and failed bookbinder) who was really just a wife.

Rosso's pride in Doris, however earnest, had taken a destructive turn; she had felt paralyzed by his expectations.

The irony was that Rosso's expectations were not as negotiable as he had imagined. That is, he had wanted Doris to mature as an artist. He *wanted* a woman with that extra layer—a gift, a sensibility, a way of seeing. Rosso was depressed to admit it but, despite her youthful ambition, Doris had turned out to be rather ordinary.

Doris was just a painter.

After all these years, Rosso *still* wanted an artist. She didn't have to work with paint. She could work with words, numbers, ideas, or bodies—for Rosso considered Charles an artist in his field.

What Rosso craved was an original mind.

A mind whose fizz and spark produces an observation whose afterglow alters every subsequent perception.

Rita had it.

Liz Taylor had enticed him with it.

He knew it when he saw it.

Rosso headed for St. John's Hospital. He was doing fifty in a twenty-five-miles-per-hour zone and pulled over the minute he saw flashing lights. In his rearview mirror, Rosso spotted Duncan, the dimwit former detective who, it now appeared, had been demoted after the Phoebe interrogation. Rosso sped ahead, giving a more worthy officer the thrill of writing a two-hundred-dollar ticket.

From his carphone, Rosso called the paging operator at St.

John's. When a scrub nurse picked up, Rosso left a message, saying that he would meet Charles after his case for lunch.

Rosso parked in the garage, took a covered bridge over to the new wing, grabbed a visitor's pass, and met Charles as he emerged from surgery in bloody scrubs and clogs.

"Let me clean up a bit," he said, smiling. He waved Rosso towards his office, leading him through endless corridors with low ceilings, strip fluorescent lighting, and black-and-beige linoleum floors whose checkerboard pattern met the ceiling at their vanishing point.

On the walls were black-and-white photographs of all the surgeons who had operated at St. John's.

Charles stopped in front of one of the many doors along the way. The plaque read Charles Dine, MD. Ph.D. General, Vascular, and Transplant Surgery. He opened the door and flipped the light switch. An intern had fallen asleep on his couch.

"Occupational hazard," Charles said.

The intern apologized and shuffled into a nearby call room. Rosso watched Charles throw his scrubs into a bin marked "Biohazard" and scanned the office as Charles showered in his private bathroom.

Above his desk were diplomas and portraits of a few pioneers in surgery—Alfred Blalock, Vivien Thomas, and John Hunter. On a bookcase filled with textbooks and the latest surgical journals were the words of the Hippocratic oath, *Primum non Nocere*, embroidered by his sister. His desk was clear, with the exception of his computer and framed pictures of Rita and his children.

Charles led Rosso to the cafeteria, a hideous expanse of beige and brown linoleum, with food that tasted no less synthetic. Just as Rosso was thinking that he could never work or eat in such an ugly place, Charles said, "Most good hospitals are dumps." He guided Rosso to the buffet line, then to a plastic booth the color of a rotting orange. "When it comes to the *great* ones," he added, "you should be suspicious of beauty."

As Rosso bit into his pizza, he noticed his friend's inquiring look. "I finally met Anne," he said.

Charles waited for him to continue.

"You might have warned me."

Charles took a stab at his salad but lost interest and looked up.

"You might have told me that you'd been intimate, don't you think?"

"I told you she was my patient."

"So you did!" Rosso exclaimed sarcastically. "Is that the same as a lover?"

Charles dropped his eyes to avoid the assault, but Rosso was going for blood. He unleashed the million angry voices that, up until now, had been jousting with Charles in his head.

"At the very least, you might have told me that the poor woman was sick, *very* sick, don't you think?"

"I didn't know you would visit her like some lovesick stalker!"

"There you go—the best defense is a good offense! Only this is not a goddamn *game!*"

"No, it's not. And I'm serious. What the hell were you doing at her house?"

"Hersh's driver got lost in her neighborhood."

"Oh *come on,* Jim!"

It suited Rosso not to recount the Bobby Orr story, since Charles would never buy it.

"Why didn't you pursue her years ago? You would have spared everyone a lot of pain."

"I had no idea I would call."

"Oh come on, Charles! You always know what you're going to do. You don't have a spontaneous bone in your body!"

"Well maybe for once I did!"

"If you did, you should have told me."

"It was a bachelor's last-minute fling. It wasn't your concern."

"And when that fling lasted throughout your marriage—"

"It didn't!"

"And when you *knew* I was pursuing a woman named Anne Farrell, was it still not my concern?"

"I wondered how you could possibly have met up with the same Anne, who was *never* a member of Smartheart and who never fancied herself Elizabeth Taylor!"

"You should have wondered aloud. You stop owning secrets when they start screwing up other people's lives!"

"The only person whose life I've screwed up is Anne's."

"Oh *really*!?" Rosso shouted. "What about your *wife*! And what about all the *crap* I've had to listen to all these years about you *knowing* it was Rita you wanted to marry?"

"I did know. I still do."

"Even if it means making her *miserable*."

Charles was silent. How could he explain the implausible truth—namely that one morning, five days after meeting Anne at the Oak Bar with Rosso, Charles had reached into his pocket and, on impulse, called the woman who had given him her phone number.

"Maybe you don't know what's going on," Charles said.

"How could I?"

"No, I mean, what's really going on."

"Fine. Tell me."

"I can't."

"Don't start this again!"

"I owe it to Rita to tell her first."

That evening, Charles retired to the office in his basement and wrote Rita a letter.

# SINGLE, WHITE CAVEMAN

*My dearest wife,*

*For some time now, I have held onto a secret which has consumed me daily. I chose not to tell you about it because I, who fear little, have been terrified that you, whom I hold most dear, would leave me or loathe me or both. And selfishly, I might add, I did not want you to take our children away—the mere thought of which makes my life not worth living.*

*Just after I met you, I met Anne Farrell. On impulse, I called a woman who had given me her number at a bar. We had one date, went canoeing twice, and grew intimate—the details of which I wish to spare you—especially since, looking back, I think the impulse was precipitated by the fear of losing you.*

*That is, you were not "in the bag," as our friend, Jim, often reminded me, and despite my bravado, I knew there was a chance that you might return to your playwright who, whatever his foibles, loved you and had more time to spend with you than I ever could.*
*A year before we married, I received a call from Anne Farrell. She had developed acute pancreatitis, an inflammation of the pancreas. By her choice—and somewhat against my will—I became her surgeon. Anne has been hanging onto her life ever since, with courage, grace, and a tenacity which, forgive me, are a few of the qualities which make me love and admire you as much as I do.*

*We all have pasts. I am not proud of mine. I cannot say that I did not love her. I can only say that we never would have succeeded as husband and wife. What's more, I loved you at the time and still love you more. Until now, I have not told you—first off, because it was an infatuation that did not continue during the course of our marriage. That said, I understand why I have seemed more remote than any husband in his right mind should be with a woman as warm and as giving as you.*

FABIENNE MARSH

*By way of explanation, I can only tell you that my feelings towards Anne grew more complicated when I was entrusted with her very survival; and my behavior, so odd around the time of our wedding, was due to Anne's failing health.*

*There is more. I don't have the heart to put the rest in writing.*

*All my love, Charles.*

## 28

Rita called Rosso and asked him to meet her for lunch at Café de la Plage. She said she needed to talk and Rosso, much in the same mood, was happy to oblige.

Since the waiter, Louis-Francois, only worked nights, they were greeted by another hyphenate, Jean-Marc-Samuel, as well as by Louis-Francois's beloved poodle, Henri-Paul, who jumped off his miniature chaise lounge to lick Rosso's face and marked his shoe with, as Jean-Marc-Samuel put it, *une petite pissette*.

After they had settled into a table overlooking the water, Rosso told Rita that he had met Anne Farrell in Boston. Since they had never had a face-to-face conversation about Anne, the only thing Rita knew was that Rosso had given up on Anne the night she had stood him up at the Ritz. With a combination of curiosity and dread, it occurred to Rita that, somehow, Rosso had met the real Anne Farrell.

"I thought you said she hadn't shown up."

"She didn't. I was in her neighborhood on business."

"How did you know where she lived?"

"I can't say." The last thing Rosso wanted Rita or anyone else to know was that he had hired Sonny the Ratter. They would think he was a complete loon.

Rita panicked, wondering if Charles had somehow given Rosso Anne's address. After a moment's thought, she ruled it out. Charles had *nothing* to gain by revealing any of this to Rosso. Besides, though Jim was unsuspicious by nature, Rita knew that with proper motivation, he was perfectly capable of finding the address himself.

"What was she like?" Rita asked.

"Quite sick. She should never have signed up with Smartheart."

"She didn't."

"She didn't what?"

"Sign up."

"How do you know?"

*Here we go*, Rita thought. She placed both elbows on the table, cupped her chin with her hands, and locked Rosso's eyes into hers. "Because I'm the Anne Farrell you met online."

"What are you talking about?"

"Do you want me to repeat what I just said?"

Rita found herself calmed by the admission, but she watched Rosso's surprise convert to anger.

"What the hell were you doing!?"

"Something desperate," she conceded. She met her friend's searing gaze with the strength and honesty which, until recently, had been the signature of her personality. "Until your birthday, I had no idea it was you."

Rita told him how, as a Smartheart employee, she had fabricated the bio of an Elizabeth Taylor look-alike and, after reading her husband's patient files, had given her the name Anne Farrell, who she had assumed was dead.

For Rosso, what Rita had done was wrong. But it was more complicated than that. He was mortified to think that, in her, he had confided the hopes and yearnings of his most private self.

Once Rita's deceit had registered, which took the better part of the lunch, there was still more which troubled him. He stared at his dessert menu, taking a moment to figure out what it was. Why, Rosso wondered, *why* hadn't Rita put an end to things once she had found out? No, it cut deeper than that. Suddenly, his feelings rioted, pulling him powerfully and simultaneously in all directions; yet, meeting Rita's gaze, he tethered them into a single question, the answer to which, he felt, would decide the future of their friendship.

"How could you agree to meet me in Boston!?"

In Rosso's tone, Rita heard disgust and disappointment, which picked at the scab of what, for Rita, was her most obscene and shameful wound. She tried to explain that she had been reeling, that she had been angry with Charles, and that she had not been thinking. When she had found the presence of mind to cancel, she had been two days late. Then she said, simply, that she was sorry, very sorry, and that she would understand if Rosso never found it in his heart to forgive her.

When Rosso arrived home, Charles was standing on his porch, suitcase in hand, saying he had nowhere to go.

"I'm unworthy," he said.

You *are* unworthy, Rosso thought, unlocking his door. And for once, Rosso, whom Charles had said was incapable of being alone, wanted nothing more than to be left in peace.

Instead, four hours after he had arrived, Charles was collapsed in Rosso's favorite chair drinking beer.

"You're pathetic!" an exasperated Rosso cried. "Call Rita and go home."

"I'm unworthy," Charles repeated.

"You *are* unworthy," Rosso agreed. He was sitting in a chair from Doris's Shaker phase, extremely uncomfortable, but, she had maintained, stylish for its pure and simple lines. So why, Rosso wondered, when they had divided up their belongings, had Doris insisted on making a "gift" of these posture-perfect, ramrods of torture?

Because, Rosso suspected, with a bloom of misanthropy now overtaking his mind like a fungus, Doris, like Rita, was full of it. Sorry to say, but that was the truth of the matter. And, however human Rita's mistake, she was far less worthy than Rosso had thought. So, really, Rosso concluded, unworthy people such as Rita and Charles *deserved* each other, *especially* if they still loved one another, which Rosso did not doubt, and doubly so if they were bound by vows. *What therefore God hath joined together, let not man put asunder.* Rosso could not have agreed more. He picked up the phone and called Rita.

"Charles wants to talk to you," he said.

Actually, Charles, now in the terminal stages of unworthiness, did not *want* to, but Rosso determined he would goddamn-well *have* to.

"Why doesn't he come home?" Rita asked.

"How the hell should I know?" an exasperated Rosso cried. "He's an incommunicative butthead who cuts people up all day and you're some overly-communicative Circe who murders men's hopes—online!"

Rita was silent for a good ten seconds. "You're right. And you have every right never to speak to me again. I'm just sorry that you've been a better friend to us than we've been to you."

"I am too," Rosso replied. He had decided there would be no point in telling Charles about Rita's role in the affair, though it was she, Rosso felt, who had most disappointed him. "If you both want to destroy your marriage, that's fine," he said evenly. "Just do me a favor and don't screw up my attempt at remarriage."

Rita laughed. She was touched by Rosso's generous display of good nature. "I love you, Jim," she said.

"Oh shut up," he said, suddenly relieved by the lowering of pretense. Then he shoved the phone into Charles's operating hand.

## 29

When Charles arrived home, he was drunk.
"I—" he began.
"You *what?*" Rita urged.
Charles could not bring himself to talk about it. Rita's heart grew heavy. She had never seen him so agitated.
"It's my fault."
"I know that," Rita said, then smiled, "but thanks for the rare admission of guilt."
"That's not what I mean."
Rita was crushed. She both needed and was owed an apology. "What do you mean, then?" she asked.
"It's my fault that Anne is sick today."
Rita was sure she had misheard.
"During the operation…"
Charles could not continue.
"During the operation, *what?*"
"During the operation…"
He could not finish.
"Charles. You've got to tell me what happened."
He mouthed something she could not make out. He was

staring right at her, pupils tiny as pin pricks. He cleared his throat and tried again. "Her kidneys failed," he said.

Rita was surprised, but in her years of being married to a surgeon, she had learned it was not an uncommon occurrence. "How is it your fault?"

"We lost pressure. She lost too much blood."

Rita was bewildered. She wanted to say, we all make mistakes, because most people do; but she knew the truth to be that Charles never did, Charles never had.

She watched his anguished face until, finally, he looked up and asked, "Do you know what it's like to *want* to be punished?"

Since Rita felt punished and could not imagine wanting the feelings she had, it was easy to reply, "No." After a moment's silence, she asked, "Isn't kidney failure always a risk?"

"Yes, but..."

"But what?"

"It's never happened in my OR and, if it had to, why did it have to happen to her?"

And with this, Charles broke down. For the next hour, he wept for all his patients, invoking those who had suffered and those who had died. With remarkable accuracy, he uttered every name, every age, every diagnosis, and every surgical effort he had made to save them. The names Rita had come across in Charles's file now emerged as full-blown people—funny, heroic, and doomed. For Charles, their bravery in the face of death was a constant source of humility and the fact that any of them had died was *his* fault, he insisted, and his *alone*.

Rita listened as Charles mourned for Anne and for his mother, who had never made it to the top of the recipient list. When he was done, when she sensed that he could say and feel no more, she asked calmly, "How is Anne now?"

He said that she was on the transplant list, that her sister had offered her own kidney.

"Does she know?"

"Know what?"

"What you just told me."

"Yes."

"And her parents?"

"I told them first."

"You told the truth."

"Yes."

"That's sufficient."

"No, it's *not*," Charles insisted. "That's the whole goddamn point! Don't you see, I deserve to be punished. I *wanted* them to file suit!"

"They chose not to."

"Yes."

"They chose to forgive you."

"Yes."

"Then you must forgive yourself."

"I can't."

"You must," she said. To Rita's own surprise, she then said something which she could not believe came from her lips, something which sounded callous but which, at the same time, she knew in her heart to be true. "You must forgive yourself," she repeated quietly and firmly. "For my sake and for the sake of your children. It's emotional suicide you're committing and it's *selfish*."

## 30

Almost a year after Rosso had joined Smartheart, Hersh approached Rosso in the office. That damn dimple of his was bouncing, which Rosso concluded meant nothing but trouble.

"Lily's thinking of registering for an Ivy League dating club named Smartheart. Heard of it?"

"Yes."

"What do you know about it?"

"I know it works for some."

"Did it work for you?"

"That's personal, sir."

"Answer me."

"No."

"No, what?"

"It didn't work for me."

"Will you talk to her about it?"

"I'd rather not."

"Talk to her," he barked. "That's an order."

On his way to meet Lily, Rosso bought a few boxed sets of country music CDs to both wallow and exult in the company of lovers done wrong. He began with "Thank God and Greyhound you're gone," moved on to "Flushed from the bathroom of your heart," and found tremendous solace in "There ain't no Queen in my king-sized bed."

Breaking into his second boxed set, Rosso smiled on hearing "If the phone doesn't ring, it's me," and was tickled out of a bad mood with "I gave her the ring, she gave me the finger." As he pulled into the parking lot behind Main Street in Westport, "Did I shave my legs for this?" somehow spoke to him—right sentiment, wrong gender.

While waiting for Lily in the coffee shop, Rosso opened his newspaper. On the front page of the National section was a picture of Lawrence Franz being taken into custody by FBI agents. Rosso recognized Mike's profile and reached for his cell phone. It was a Saturday, but Rosso knew Mike would be in his office. His indefatigable dedication put him in front of his computer six days a week.

"I'm reading the paper and looking at Franz in cuffs. Nice work."

"Just givin' the press their photo op," Mike said. "Thanks for the logs."

After Rosso hung up, he was heartened that his long-standing friendship with Mike, however monosyllabic, had produced such noble results. On the margins of his newspaper, next to the closing prices on the New York Stock Exchange, Rosso made a list of his friends and concluded that, with the exception of Charles and professional acquaintances like Mike and Sonny, he had none. In addition to the non-essential friendships Doris had nixed, Rosso, over the years, had trimmed a few buddies of his own. Gone were those indiscriminate pairings that, in his early twenties, had Rosso doing shots when he rarely drank to excess or smoking a cigar after dinner when he normally passed on Cubans. First-tier friendships had remained immutable, but anyone below the third tier had been bombed as decisively as suspicious baggage at Heathrow.

The problem was that Rosso had eliminated all those relationships which, however ignoble, get single people through their day. Since then, many of Rosso's castaways had gotten married and had kids; and now, just when he needed them most, he was on *their* termination list.

Non-essential friendship.

We'll call you.

Lower fifth tier.

Rosso looked up from his short list and prayed that Lily would not show up. He resented having his personal calendar, however pathetically uncommitted, shackled by his boss's daughter.

He watched the various women entering the coffee shop—each one more intriguing, pleasing, or just plain to his taste than the last. Inside, one beautiful and apparently kind woman handed a biscuit to her baby. She was married to a short, bald man twice her age—not that there was anything wrong with him—except, as one of Rosso's harsher country tune's put it, "You're the reason our children are ugly."

By the window, another woman sat alone, a natural beauty who Rosso decided would look great in a canoe. When she glanced at her watch, Rosso wanted to see who she was waiting for. If he turned out to be a toad, Rosso would kill himself, a sacrifice he was now willing to make for *all* single men—nay, for all single people who navigated the rough seas and treacherous shoals of love. When the man walked in, Rosso cried, "Ugh," obviously unable to conceal his disgust. The woman heard him and smiled in the direction of the man who had entered.

He was the opposite of what Rosso had pictured—tall and, well, pretty, with hazel eyes set deeply in his tanned face. To Rosso, who was a champion of hygiene, the fellow looked too clean—so clean as to be sexless, with sunglasses resting in his curly brown hair and a tennis sweater carefully tied over his shoulders.

"What a dunce!" the woman at the window whispered conspiratorially.

Rosso started. "What's that?"

"I said, what a dunce. You know—a male bimbo. Nice to look at, but not enough mystery, shadow, and intellect."

Rosso was dumbfounded, but a couple of minutes later, he snapped to and seized the opportunity to clear up a few questions he had—and conceded he might *always* have—about women.

"I wonder if you might answer a question related to your observations," Rosso offered a bit tentatively.

"Sure," the woman said sweetly.

"What do women like you want?"

The woman laughed. But oh that laugh, rich and warm as the sand in a spangled surf. This was Venus, herself, stranded in a Westport coffee shop!

In the moments that followed, Rosso begged Lily to hold off from showing up. That way, he would receive an answer from the very kind of woman he had always wanted—brainy, funny, original, and, honestly, last of all, attractive. Okay, in this particular case, his ideal. And this vital information would come *before* any catching, preening, watching, and wanting—that is, before the very sport of dating and mating compromised the information.

The woman's long, glossy black eyelashes dipped to ponder Rosso's question, as if the answer lay in her latte. Just then, a woman Rosso knew would be Lily threatened the moment with her loud and bossy Birkenstocks. He would *never* get his answer, he moaned to himself. And he desperately wanted the response from a single woman—not from Charles; not from a married woman like Rita; but from a woman still in the game.

"I can only speak for myself," the woman began. "I would like a man who is funny, confident, smart, sexy, open-minded, and kind."

"What about rich? Don't all women want rich?"

"As I said, I can only speak for myself. But I would assume that a man with those qualities would have no trouble making a living in whatever he decided to do."

Rosso was buoyed by her confidence in men, by her very love, understanding, and generosity of spirit towards her most opposite gender. He decided that the world needed more women like her.

In an instant, he summoned forth a picture of their life together. Two months of wild sex followed by their first child. After that, he would work, cook, change diapers, scrub floors, and even iron. *Whatever it took* to make this woman the mother of his children.

"I assume," this philosophical Venus continued, "that men are looking for the same thing. The only difference being that some men would feel threatened once they got it. Which is to say that women seek their peers or better and men often settle for less."

The Grape-Nut munching, dung-scraping Birkenstocker stopped by Rosso's table.

"You must be Lily," he said politely, resigned to his fate.

Venus started to laugh. Only now she laughed in a manner Rosso found raucous, inappropriate, and quite possibly mean-spirited. Suddenly, Rosso felt protective of this chubby, pimply, post-graduate boss's daughter because, despite his flaws, he considered himself first and foremost an officer and a gentleman.

He turned towards the woman he now suspected was a Venus flytrap, a glacial goddess—theoretically brilliant and versed in human affairs, but cold as the Volga near Novosibirsk.

"Why are you laughing? " Rosso asked.

Her laughter proved so infectious that, to Rosso's irritation, a few caffeine-drinkers started joining in.

Rosso turned to the young Ph.D, the boss's daughter, now standing by his side. He read sorrow in her eyes and futility in her soul—all of which, from *her* perspective, could be construed only as a look of simple petulance.

"Are you done with your cinnamon?" she asked.

"Sure," a puzzled Rosso replied.

"Can I have it?"

As Rosso reached to pass her the shaker, he felt a tap on his shoulder. When he turned, he saw Venus by the window smiling.

"My name is Lily," she said. "You must be Jim."

Rosso stared without seeing and with still less comprehension. "My father's Bob Hersh," she said.

"Your father?" Rosso said.

"Yes."

"My boss."

"That's right."

He scanned her flawless face, one he found very easy to get lost in, bypassed her eyes, and x-rayed her very soul. This is the woman I'm going to marry, he said to himself. He was as certain as the sun, as grounded as the earth, as calm as the waters of the most peaceful bay, and imbued with the truisms of every sappy song that had ever played on AM radio. Despite a year filled with psychos, colossally flawed judgment, and the hope-snuffing vaporization of Elizabeth Taylor, Rosso marveled that he, James Adams Rosso, was finally experiencing a moment of clarity known only to the Charles Dines of the world.

With one troubling exception.

That is, he honestly did not know which would be more frightening: to start dating again, or to have Bob Hersh as a father-in-law.

## ABOUT THE AUTHOR

**Fabienne Marsh** is the author of four novels and numerous works of non-fiction. Her film credits have appeared on dozens of documentary films and she has taught writing at both Johns Hopkins University and the University of Minnesota.

Marsh grew up in Edgemont, New York, the daughter of a French mother and a father of Irish-English descent. At Williams College, she studied with John Gardner and took a double major in English and political science. After a five-year stint with the documentary unit at ABC News, during which she enrolled in the Columbia University Writer's Program under a Woolrich Fellowship, Marsh won a journalism fellowship and studied international relations at The London School of Economics. Upon her return to the States, Marsh worked on television documentaries, while publishing her critically-acclaimed novels, *Long Distances* and *The Moralist of the Alphabet Streets*, followed by her third novel, *Single, White, Cave Man*.

Marsh has served as a writer-consultant for Nickelodeon, HBO, Turner Broadcasting and Public Broadcasting (WNET and WETA). Her lighter works of non-fiction include *Dave'sWorld*, with co-author Michael Cader about David Letterman, and the coffee-table book, *Saturday Night Live: The First Twenty Years*, for which Marsh interviewed Candice Bergen, Steve Martin, Chris Rock, and other cast members.

Marsh's freelance articles have appeared in The New York Times, the Chicago Tribune, The Economist, the International Herald Tribune, Southbay magazine and Poetry Review (London). Her radio essays aired on MPR's "Marketplace" and WHYY. Marsh has taught literature and creative writing at Loyola (Baltimore) and for three years, she served as the Journalism Advisor for the Chadwick School in California.

Marsh is currently living in the South Bay of Los Angeles. You can keep up with her new releases and special events on her Authors Guild website: https://www.fabiennemarsh.com/